Splinter

A DIVERSE RETELLING OF
THE LEGEND OF SLEEPY HOLLOW

JASPER HYDE

Copyright © 2023 by Jasper Hyde | Georgina Kiersten

All rights reserved.

No part of this publication may be reproduced, distributed, or transmitted in any form or by any means, including photocopying, recording, or other electronic or mechanical methods, without the prior written permission of the publisher, except as permitted by U.S. copyright law. For permission requests, contact Georgina Kiersten at georginakiersten@gmail.com.

The story, all names, characters, and incidents portrayed in this production are fictitious. No identification with actual persons (living or deceased), places, buildings, and products is intended or should be inferred.

Book Cover by Georgina Kiersten

Edited by Ivy Quinn and Gabriel Hargrave

Visual Assets by Adobe Stock

Paperback ISBN: 9798223075240

Contents

Epigraph	VI
Dedication	VIII
Author's Note	X
Subscribe to My Newsletter	XIV
Prologue	I
1. Chapter One	9
2. Chapter Two	17
3. Chapter Three	25
4. Chapter Four	33
5. Chapter Five	43
6. Chapter Six	53
7. Chapter Seven	65
8. Chapter Eight	71
9. Chapter Nine	83
10. Chapter Ten	91

11.	Chapter Eleven	99
12.	Chapter Twelve	105
13.	Chapter Thirteen	115
14.	Chapter Fourteen	127
15.	Chapter Fifteen	141
16.	Chapter Sixteen	147
17.	Chapter Seventeen	157
18.	Chapter Eighteen	167
19.	Chapter Nineteen	173
20.	Chapter Twenty	181

Epilogue	189
Bonus Chapter	195
Acknowledgements	197
About the Author	199
The Magnificent Engine	201
Support These Amazing Filipino Authors	203
Leave A Review	205

" All these, however, were mere terrors of the night, phantoms of the mind that walk in darkness; and though he had seen many spectres in his time, and been more than once beset by Satan in divers shapes, in his lonely pre-ambulations, yet daylight put an end to all these evils; and he would have passed a pleasent life of it, in despite of the devil and all his works, if his path had not been crossed by a being that causes more perplexity to mortal man than ghosts, goblins, and the whole race of witches put together, and that was - a woman."

—— Washington Irving, The Legend of Sleepy Hollow

I dedicate this book to Nicole Beharrie. Her portrayal of Abigail Grace Mills opened the doors for so many of us and showed everyone that Black women can be not only beautiful but brilliant, resilient, strong, and vulnerable all at the same time. And I also dedicate this book to Black women everywhere! Women who had to make their own magic in a world that constantly underestimated them. This is for you!

AUTHOR'S NOTE

I want to thank you so much for purchasing my diverse Sleepy Hollow retelling Splinter. This book has been a two-year labor of love and I'm so happy that I am able to finally to be able to share it with you.

Before you read this book there are a few things I want to warn you about. If you are from the Hudson Valley area you will notice right off the bat that my version of Sleepy Hollow and the real Sleepy Hollow are two very different places. I tried to keep to the soul of the town and I was lucky to get consultation from real-life residents of Sleepy Hollow and Tarrytown.

However, I put my own spin on the town and they are things that are moved around for the purpose of this story. Related to this is the use of alternate history. In particular Revolutionary War history. Things might be incorrect and I did a lot of that on purpose because I wanted to write a slight alternate history.

And finally, a lot of this book is pulled from my own experience. Although I'm not demisexual, I am an aromantic asexual. I also have dyslexia, autism, and ADHD.

I'm also not a medical examiner or any type of medical professional. I know that I probably got a few things wrong here or there.

The last thing I didn't take from my own lived experience was Ichabod's Filipino Heritage. My version of Ichabod Crane is a biracial Filipino (Filipino/White). I did as much research as I could on my own but I also got two Filpino sensitivity readers to go over this book P.K. Reeves and Cat Giraldo.

Unfortunately, I know that even though I made my best effort to make this book a safe space for Filipino readers, I know that some things could have fallen through the cracks. If you find something offensive or harmful please let me know by georgina kiersten@gmail.com and I will do my best to correct it.

Content Warnings

Police
Infidelity (brief mention)
Bullying (brief mention)
Decapitation
Misogynoir (implied)
Colorism (implied)
Racism (implied)
Gore
Blood
Explicit Violence
Slavery

Subscribe to My Newsletter

Receive early access to upcoming book ARCs, news about my other projects, and episodes for my upcoming serials. You will also get exclusive discounts, behind-the-scenes sneak peeks, and more! All you have to do is to sign up for my FREE newsletter!

Prologue

Sleepy Hollow 1781

Death was in the air tonight. It came upon the residents of Sleepy Hollow at the sound of thundering hooves. Tucked tightly in their beds, all they could do was wait. Yet, beyond their doors, there was one resident who didn't heed the warnings. The clock tower tolled midnight and on to the dirt streets of the town, a person rode through the streets of the town. In the moonlight, if one was curious enough to peek outside would see the blue tattered coat of a colonial soldier.

The manifestation of their dread would have been witnessed by the curious onlooker if they had stayed for a moment longer - a huge man riding a ghostly white horse, with an axe that gleamed with malice.

Luckily, the majority of inhabitants were oblivious to the danger that swiftly passed by their homes.

To reach safety, the colonial soldier could only ride and hope. They tightly held the reins, urging their horse to go faster as their pursuer closed in on them.

The soldier and the horseman rode across the gristmill, then past the brick and white painted steeple of the old Dutch church, the Pocantico River, and finally out into the forest. "Only a little further." The soldiers muttered, their legs pressing hard against the horse and gratefully the horse obeyed and increased its pace. Sadly, the soldier knew they couldn't maintain this speed for long.

The soldier noticed the horseman in their peripheral vision, but the sound of their own heart pounding drowned out the horses' hooves as they rushed across the crimson-colored bridge.

"Come on," the soldier muttered under his breath. "We are going to make it." It wasn't just their life on the line, but thousands of slaves whose freedom depended on their success.

Failure was not an option.

Their horse reared up, a shrill sound coming from it and then the soldier was being thrown off the horse and onto the ground. The next thing the soldier could see was an axe protruding from his horse. The soldier looked up and there the horseman was getting off his steed and heading towards them.

The soldier didn't know how they got the strength but they managed to get up on their feet. Blood trickled into their eyes, and their legs screamed with pain. Their long curly hair spilled around their face further hampering their view but they knew their death was swift in coming. The soldier got stiffly on their feet and ran into the forest.

The forest was eerily quiet and still as the soldier ran but they knew the horseman wasn't far behind. Branches snagged into their hair, slicing across the soldier's brown vulnerable skin as they ran. The soldier was no stranger to pain and they would rather suffer these injuries than be caught. If they were caught it would be the end for not only them but the colonies.

They had to survive, they had to make it to safety.

The soldier darted out from the corpse of trees into a clearing and waiting for them was a group of figures in dark robes. The soldier slowed to a stop, their eyes going wide, and then suddenly they were being lifted off the ground by the throat. Their eyes went wide as they turned to see the Horseman's hands around his neck.

Heat rushed through the soldier's body so hot that it felt that could scorch their very bones. *"Furche,"* The soldier managed to squeeze through the tight vice around their throat and then the soldier was suddenly released and slumped to the ground.

The soldier coughed, their bodies shuttering as they desperately gasped for air. The solider turned and jumped as they saw the head of the Horseman lying beside them. They cried out and scrabbled away from it. A hand grabbed their shoulder and jerked away and there standing in front of the soldier was a robed figure.

"Come, we don't have much time," said a rough masculine voice.

The soldier hurried to follow their savior noticing the robed figures had formed a half circle around the horseman. The robed individuals chanted as they formed an invisible shield with a glowing light emanating from their fingertips. The soldier managed to pass it easily, but the Horseman's headless body rose to chase and slammed against it.

With the soldier and his savior now part of the group, they faced the Horseman. The soldiers' pain dissipated as they chanted in unison, fueled by the fire in their veins:

delme bierme elementse stende plon avna ,

te e aide bierme horseman s oso ,

suande atme , nuf, plin e frue ,

bierme nu s voin does cuin falter bierme angique slides mue ,

bierme freunde is sprunge ,

suande these uordse uepre ien crin

The horseman's body was slashed, resembling a shattered pane of glass. His wounds glowed in a brilliant vermilion color, and the body fell apart piece by piece onto the ground. The pieces astonishingly burst into flame and dissolved into ash.

For hours under the full moon, they chanted, but the head of the horseman remained intact. Its eyes gazed at them, devoid of life. The soldier thought they would fold under the strain of the spell as time stretched on and on.

Then they finally stopped, and the soldier collapsed on the ground.

"Mathilde."

They slowly cracked open their eyes and their kneeling above them was a familiar and dear face. A man who had dark brown skin, short kinky hair, a trimmed beard, and kind almond-shaped dark eyes looked at Mathilde with concern.

"Pieter."

Mathilde reached out, their fingers caressed the face of their beloved. Out of nowhere, a fog descended upon them and they felt detached from their body, as if they were observing from a distance. Mathilde could only stare in amazement as they opened their mouth and spoke.

"*A whitewood tree grown in chains,*

will wither and dwindle,

a branch will fall and split in two.

The first will be lost to the allure of milky petals

The second will be drenched in crimson, burning with poena's song,

the obsidian pawn will rise again,"

"*two and two and two again,*

one choice will have to be made,

and a chosen will rise,

will the branches will twist and warp,

together as one, slaying the pawn,

and a new age will be born?"
"Or the branches will break and splinter,
the yew with wither and die,
the tendrils of chaos and death will rise and eclipse.
all will be lost?"

Then abruptly, reality snapped back in place and Mathilde gasped and looked up at Pieter and then over to where the head of the Horseman lay. They stood up and went over to the head.

"This isn't the end, isn't it?"

"No," Mathilde closed their eyes and shuttered. The others rushed towards Mathilde, pointing at the head and speaking in panicked voices.

"What about our deal with Benjamin Franklin? A member of the robed group inquired as Mathilde gazed at the coven that had put themselves in danger for this opportunity. Mathilde risked their life and the life of their coven to bait the trap and capture the Horseman.

"He is...gone for now." Mathilde stood rigid, their chin stubbornly held high. "We did what we could."

Pieter came forward and took Mathilde's hand. "No one will be safe when The Horseman returns."

"What should do?"

"The Great Mother has prophesized the coming of a chosen one, and we must trust Iurti's words," Mathilde insisted determinedly.

And Pieter stood beside them, grasping Mathlide's hand and squeezing it as they looked at their companions. "We must have faith."

One

A Rude Awakening

Drusilla awoke to the sound of something crashing to the floor. She sat up in bed, her heart pounding in her chest. For a moment, Drusilla believed she was still standing in the forest clearing. She could almost feel the heaviness and comfort of Pieter's hand in hers.

Drusilla pried her shaking fingers from the sheets and reached out to turn on the light. Her eyes immediately went to the shards of her father's favorite antique porcelain vase on the floor. *How in the hell did that break?* Maybe she accidentally knocked it over in her sleep?

It had survived centuries, only to get destroyed. Drusilla got a lump in her throat and her eyes stung with unshed tears. Her father would have been at the waste.

"I knew I should have put it downstairs."

Logically, Drusilla knew her father was dead and that he would storm into her room and he wouldn't be giving her one of his long-winded lectures. I would do anything to have him back for just one more day, even if it meant breaking everything in this damn house. It had been five months since his passing, and everyone said it would get easier with time. But Drusilla was still waiting for the day she didn't expect him to turn the corner, a smile on his face.

Enough of that, Drusilla thought to herself as she firmly shoved her grief and anguish down. With a sigh, she gathered a bucket, dustpan, and broom and started cleaning up the mess.

Drusilla hated this time of year. Sleepy Hollow seemed to lose itself to Halloween madness, and the Headless Horseman was the town's favorite specter.

And even with all her logic, Drusilla couldn't quite escape that madness, even her dreams. It seeped through the walls, haunting her. She'd tried medication, therapy–hell, working herself to exhaustion. But every night when Drusilla closed her eyes, she would be back on her horse being chased through the streets of Sleepy Hollow.

Drusilla was just sweeping up the last of the mess and reverently placing the shards in the bucket, hoping to repair it later, when her phone rang.

"Van Tassel!"

"Doc." Sheriff Thornton's voice was gruff. "We got a body over in Tarrytown."

Drusilla rubbed her eyes and barely suppressed a sigh as the Sheriff gave her the address. She reassured him she would be there as soon as she could and hung up. Drusilla looked at the time on her phone screen. It was five-thirty a.m.

Well, it wasn't like I was getting any more sleep, anyway. Drusilla shook her head. Besides, she would rather work than have to wait out the rest of the morning in the too eerie quiet of the manor.

Drusilla had fully expected to be called in earlier. She was on call today, and being on call during the graveyard shift meant they often woke her up in the middle of the night.

Drusilla quickly stripped and dressed in her usual uniform of simple blue hospital scrubs, her funky red and white argyle socks, and her black Chucks–her only minor rebellion against her boss's strict dress code.

She took off her black bonnet, and her copper curls, done up in thick twists that fell to her shoulders. She didn't have time to undo them and arrange them in her usual twist-out, so she just gave them a quick check in the mirror, then hurried out of her room and down the grand staircase into the living room.

Stopping at the mantle over the fireplace, Drusilla touched the carved cow horn that had been used in the Revolutionary War. It had been one of her father's rare auction finds, and touching it made her feel closer to him.

Wish me luck, Dad, Drusilla thought to herself, shaking her head at her ridiculous superstition.

With a sigh, she hurried out into the darkness of the early morning. Drusilla could see Hobbs, the farm's foreman, already out and about tending to the horses. She gave the elderly white man a wave before hurrying into the garage.

Drusilla slid behind the wheel of her sleek black Lincoln Continental and sped down the long drive and onto the narrow road that led into town.

Traffic was almost non-existent, as most of Sleepy Hollow was just now waking to start another day. Crossing the narrow boundary from The Hollow into Tarrytown took almost no time at all.

The crime scene was a quaint gray and white cottage on top of a hill near the Tarrytown Music Hall. As Drusilla pulled up the street, the flashing red and blue lights of the police cars cut through the darkness of early morning. Standing on the sidewalk were neighbors with their phones out, recording the chaos, and she even spotted Estelle Cruz, a reporter from The Hollow Herald, in the crowd.

Deaths like these always affected small towns, and what affected Tarrytown always affected Sleepy Hollow. Until 1997, Sleepy Hollow was a wealthy historic area in North Tarrytown, but for all intents and purposes, the two towns were indistinguishable to outsiders.

"Did they call the entire county?" Drusilla muttered to herself as she counted how deputies were swarming around the house.

There were too many police cars blocking the roads, so she had to park a few blocks away. With a put-upon sigh, Drusilla got out of her car and opened the enormous trunk. She grabbed her white coveralls and slipped them on, then pulled the hood over her twists and put on her white medical mask. Drusilla grabbed the rest of her equipment and started the long trek up the hill.

Drusilla was sweaty and panting for breath by the time she finally made it to the cottage. With a sigh of relief, she adjusted her bag and pulled up the yellow tape that marked off the perimeter.

"Excuse me!"

She looked up to see a white deputy running to her. He was tall and lanky with mousy brown hair poking out from under his large-brimmed tan hat. Drusilla frowned. In her line of work, Drusilla was very familiar with most of the law enforcement in the area, so she was pretty sure this guy was fresh out of the academy. Drusilla looked at the badge and saw the name "Hansen" printed on it.

Deputy Hansen put out his hand. "You can't go beyond this point."

Drusilla barely stopped herself from rolling her eyes, and she gestured to her coveralls. "I'm the medical examiner."

He frowned and looked her up and down. Drusilla was a petite dark-skinned woman. It didn't matter that she was a thirty-four-year-old forensic pathologist who'd graduated Magna Cum Laude from Cornell. Most men in law enforcement only saw her as a Black girl playing dress up.

Drusilla sighed and, without a word, handed him her badge.

"Let me check with my superior."

Of course, you will, Drusilla thought snidely.

She was hot and sweaty, and her equipment bags were heavy. All she wanted to do was get to work. She took a deep breath. kept her professional mask on, and just nodded. It wouldn't do to give these people any more reason to doubt her.

"Doc!" She jumped when she saw an older white man walking over to them. "Took you long enough."

Sheriff Carson Thornton was a tall, heavy-set man with short black hair and a worn, craggy face. Usually, the Sheriff had a jovial air around him, but this morning, his mouth was set in a grim line.

Drusilla adjusted the straps of her bag again. "I'm sorry, Sheriff. I had some trouble entering the crime scene." She turned to the deputy, whose face was turning the shade of a ripe tomato.

Sheriff Thornton patted Hansen on the back. "Don't mind Bryce. He's a little eager."

Drusilla said nothing and dipped under the tape. At the door, she slipped on blue shoe covers and her latex gloves.

"Hey, wait!" The Sheriff ran over to her. "Before you go in, there's something I need to tell you."

"I'm a big girl. I think I can handle it." Drusilla brushed him off. She was more than ready to get to work.

Drusilla marched into what had been once a typical suburban home but was now complete mayhem. The sofa and chairs were overturned, with deep gashes in the fabric. Glass from various shattered picture frames was scattered across the floor. In the center of the chaos, lying between two pieces of what had once been a coffee table, was a headless body lying in a pool of their own blood.

She quickly crossed the room, carefully stepping over the detritus to where a disembodied head lay on the floor. Then she paled, her eyes fixed on the all-too-familiar face. She'd know Denis Carter anywhere, even in his current unfortunate state.

"Doc?" Sherrif Thornton asked. "You alright?"

Drusilla nodded, turning away from the macabre display. Her eyes landed on a tiny table sitting in the corner. It was one of the few things still intact in the chaos of the living room. And perched on top of it was a silver-framed photo. In the shot was a group of smiling teenagers who had their arms around each other, grinning into the camera.

And right there, next to a very whole and alive Denis Carter, was her sister, Katrina Van Tassel.

Two

HERE COMES TROUBLE

"*Clumsy bitch!*"

Drusilla remembered Denis Carter sneering down at her when she'd accidentally bumped into him and spilled the wine she'd been nursing all over his designer shirt. Which, he'd informed her snidely, cost more than her car.

It had been the night of her sister's engagement party. Drusilla remembered her sister throwing her wide, pleading eyes and her fiance Brom's tight, foreboding expression. In the end, Drusilla simply apologized and walked away.

Turns out, that was the last time she would ever speak to Denis Carter.

And now, Drusilla stood inches away from Denis' severed head. His face was a permanent testament to the few moments of terror before he was murdered. She'd hated him for years; hell, she wasn't too fond of any of her sister and brother-in-law's friends. But Drusilla never wanted him dead.

"Drusilla!"

She shook her head and turned back to Sheriff Thornton, who looked like he'd been trying to gain her attention for a while now.

"Are you alright?" he asked. "Do I need to call Willard?"

Drusilla took a deep breath and then another. She shoved all her feelings in the same mental box she'd always shoved the rest of her inconvenient emotions.

I don't have time for this!

Drusilla was the youngest medical examiner in the county's history, and at the end of the day, she was still a goddamn professional, despite everyone in Westchester County thinking she was some naïve little country girl. With the ease of long practice, Drusilla pushed away her shock. She ignored the look of concern Sheriff Thornton gave her and got to work. She would treat this body like any other and would deal with the emotional fallout later.

Sheriff Thorton coughed. "We can skip the introduction if—"

Drusilla raised a hand. "No, we go by the book. Give me the rundown."

Sheriff Thornton sighed and flipped open his notebook. "Denis Carter, heir to the Carter's real estate fortune. He was married to Saundra Carter, who works as an executive at Nordstrom, and they don't have any kids."

Drusilla started by taking the temperature of the room before she took out her camera and began snapping photos. It was standard procedure for her to make sure she got an accurate record of the crime before she made her way back to the body.

"It was called in by some neighbors," Sheriff Thornton continued. "They heard gunshots. One of the neighbors swore up and down that they saw a headless man flee the scene on a white horse."

Drusilla snorted. "People love to blame everything on the Horseman this time of year. Did someone break into the general store? It was the Horseman. A pet goes missing? It was the Horseman. Hell, the other day, Mr. Richards told me that he thinks the Horseman has been stealing his prize pumpkins."

Sheriff Thornton snorted back. "Richards needs to lay off the weed."

Drusilla shook her head and finished taking photos. She wasn't the type of person to depend on crime scene technicians to be as thorough as her. It sounded arrogant, but Drusilla had learned the hard way to keep her own records.

"It looks like the perpetrator broke down the door and then had a confrontation with Carter," she said.

"The neighbor said she heard three gunshots."

"Did the technician already bag the gun?"

"Yeah." Sheriff Thornton looked down at his notebook. "It's a Glock 19."

"I'll make sure to swab for gunshot residue, then," Drusilla said as she put her camera in her bag, discarded her gloves, and put on a fresh pair. "Did they find the bullets?"

"No." The Sheriff frowned. "They're still looking."

As Drusilla examined the body, she said, "There was obviously a struggle."

She studied the severe abrasions on Carter's chest and arms. The victim's skin was starting to look pale and waxy. Drusilla checked the temperature of the room again, scribbling it down in her notepad.

"But the way the blood is pooling and with the position of the victim's head..." she mused aloud.

Drusilla took a deep breath and swallowed all of her feelings as she went back to the head. She examined the eyes, the mouth, and then, finally, the severance point. After checking the head's temperature, she once again measured the room's temp.

"With the condition of the body," Drusilla said, standing up and shaking her head, "my preliminary estimation of time of death was around four a.m."

"Okay." Thornton nodded and then looked back at the body and snorted. "And we all know what the cause of death was."

"I'd rather not make assumptions," Drusilla said coolly. "That's how mistakes are made."

Sheriff Thornton's eyebrows rose, but he thankfully didn't seem to take offense. He tapped his pen against his notebook. "Is there anything here we can use to catch this son of a bitch?"

Drusilla wrapped the victim's hands in bags to preserve any evidence and waved to her assistants. Kyndall, her head assistant, nodded to her as she hurried over to them with the stretcher. She threw Drusilla an apologetic look for being so late, but Drusilla waved her off. Kyndall and the others carefully picked up the body and placed it inside the black body bag.

"Well, I'm off." Drusilla nodded to Sheriff Thorton. "I'll email you my final results as soon as I can."

The Sheriff tipped his hat at her. "I appreciate that." His phone rang, and he took it out, frowning at the display. "Fuck, it's the Mayor."

Drusilla gave him a sympathetic look and turned to go. She stepped out onto the front porch and took a deep breath of the cool morning air.

The sun had finally risen, and pink and orange hues were painted across the sky. The crowd had thinned a bit, which meant the neighbors had finally gotten bored with the drama. A few reporters were trying to press forward to get a sound bite from her.

"Can you tell us about the murder?"

"Is there a serial killer on the loose?"

Drusilla ignored the questions as she searched for the quickest way through the crowd to her car. Her eyes caught sight of the most striking man she had ever seen. Drusilla's heart sped up as she felt something hot zip down her spine and tug at her core. The man was tall, standing heads above most people in the crowd. Yet, that wasn't the only thing that made him stand out. He was one of the few people of color in the crowd, with tan-brown skin and fox-shaped eyes.

With his designer peacoat and artfully arranged scarf, he looked like he belonged in Brooklyn more than in her cozy little seaside town.

A tape recorder was suddenly shoved in her face.

"Dr. Van Tassel, a statement, please?" Estelle Cruz demanded. The younger woman was relentless. People underestimated her age and her height, as she was only slightly taller than Drusilla at 5'4ft, with light bronze skin, a short black mullet, and Estelle's adorable elfin features framed by big black round glasses.

Drusilla had enough experience with the reporter to understand that Estelle would never give up on a juicy story. Unfortunately for Drusilla, the murder of a Carter was as juicy as it gets. She pushed the recorder out of her face. "No comment," Drusilla replied curtly before shoving her way through the crowd and the reporters.

An agonized scream cut through the air, and Drusilla spun around to see Saundra Carter being held back by the same deputy who'd stopped her earlier.

"Let me go!" Saundra cried, tears streaking down her pale face. "That's my goddamn husband!"

Drusilla knew that she should help Saundra. She was her sister's best friend, and she'd just lost her husband. But still, Drusilla hesitated. Denis and Saundra had fought like cats and dogs; their fights were legendary in the Hollow. But the one thing the couple did agree on was that they both hated Drusilla. And she was pretty sure her face was the last one the grieving widow would want to see now.

Drusilla pushed past the last of the spectators and hurried down the hill to where her car was parked. She pulled out her keys and unlocked the door.

"Wait!" a deep masculine voice called out.

"No comment." Drusilla gritted her teeth as she yanked open the door.

"Drusilla."

Drusilla went still, her heart pounding in her chest. The clipped British accent was achingly familiar but had grown deep with age. However, this was one man's voice that she could never seem to forget, no matter how hard she'd tried.

This man, a ghost straight out of her teenage fantasies, was so close that she could smell the earthy scent of sandalwood and vellum.

"Drusilla," he called for her softly, his breath tickling the back of her neck.

She barely repressed a shudder at the way his mouth said her name as if it was almost a physical caress. Drusilla snapped her eyes closed and prayed that this was just some delusion brought up by the traumatic crime scene and a lack of sleep.

"Ichabod Crane," Drusilla said, taking a shaky breath as she finally turned around.

Drusilla couldn't believe that she hadn't immediately recognized him when she saw him in the crowd. Those damnable fox-shaped eyes cut through her with their intensity. Up close, Ichabod's hazel eyes were gray-green with flecks of gold. Their time apart from each other hadn't lessened the effect those eyes had on her.

Drusilla looked away, her own eyes tracing the features of his face: sharp cheekbones, neatly trimmed mustache, and full lips–lips that she viscerally remembered the taste of.

Drusilla opened her mouth to speak, but nothing came out. What could she say to the man who had broken her heart, the man whose presence lingered long after he left?

And now, sixteen years later, Ichabod Crane had finally returned to Sleepy Hollow.

Three

Broken Threads

"It's *Doctor* Van Tassel now." Drusilla crossed her arms.

Ichabod lifted an eyebrow, and she just glared up at him. Why did he have to be so fucking tall? It made it all too easy for him to loom over her.

"Why are you here?" she asked.

"My mother still lives here."

As if that had ever mattered to Ichabod. While Drusilla hadn't spoken to Ichabod for over a decade, she could never shut the door on her relationship with Analyn Crane. Over the years, the two women had forged a tight bond, and Analyn had become the mother she'd never had.

It infuriated her to no end that this inconsiderate jackass would make his aging mother take the train to the city to see her son whenever he took time off his busy schedule gallivanting across the globe. Meanwhile, Drusilla's mother abandoned their family at the age of six and never came back.

"As nice as it was to see you again, Crane," Drusilla replied through gritted teeth, "I need to get back to work."

Drusilla turned around and went to open her car door again, but he reached out and grabbed her arm. She barely repressed the shiver of the warmth at the feel of his calloused fingertips.

"Drus—" She glared up at him, and he coughed and jerked away before trying again. "Doctor, I heard that you found Denis Carter's decapitated body. Can you tell me more about it?"

Drusilla narrowed her eyes. How did he know that? Was one of the deputies spilling information to civilians? She had to talk to Sheriff Thornton about that. He was getting way too lenient with his staff.

"That's confidential information," she told him.

"Any answers you have could help stop the Horseman."

Drusilla shook her head and gave an incredulous laugh. He still believed in the supernatural? She had hoped that he had grown up. Apparently not.

"I didn't know you were a cop."

Ichabod huffed. "I'm not."

"Then you have no right to that information." Drusilla turned again.

"Please," Ichabod pleaded. "Surely, you are worried about Katrina with a killer on the loose."

"You have metrics fucking tons of audacity to even mention Katrina" Drusilla glared at him, " I just want you to know that I'm working to keep this county safe for Katrina and everyone else. Leave the real police work to the professionals and stop playing Sherlock Holmes.

"Why are you being so bloody difficult?"

Drusilla shook her head. "You got a lot of fucking nerve to ask me anything after what you did."

"What *I* did?" Ichabod chuckled. "You love to play innocent, don't you?"

Drusilla snarled, "What the fuck is that supposed to mean?"

Ichabod opened his mouth, closed it, and then took a deep breath. "I'm sorry. I'm just trying to help—"

"The only way you can help, Crane, is to leave this to the authorities. They don't need an amateur screwing up this investigation." Drusilla slipped behind the wheel and slammed the door in his face.

Reveling in Ichabod's obvious frustration, she smiled smugly to herself as she drove away.

The rest of the day didn't get any better after that. Drusilla didn't have time to stop by The Grindhouse Cafe for a cinnamon dolce latte but instead had to deal with the awful sludge from the break room. As one of the few full-time medical examiners on staff, Drusilla was slammed with most of the county's enormous backlog of bodies and paperwork. Drusilla much preferred the bodies to all the tedious paperwork. And in the tiny breaks she managed to squeeze in during the day, Drusilla tried to call and text her sister.

Her calls went straight to voicemail.

The two sisters had always had an unsteady relationship, which came with being polar opposites of each other. But lately, the rift between them seemed to get bigger and bigger by the day.

This radio silence didn't sit well with her.

The news about Denis' murder must have spread all over the county by now. After everything that had happened in the last two years, Drusilla didn't know if Katrina could deal with another loss.

Correction. Drusilla knew damn well that she couldn't.

By the time Drusilla got to Carter's body near the end of the day, Thornton and her supervisor, Dr. Willard, were pressing for an official cause of death.

In short, Dr. Drusilla Van Tassel was too damn busy to give a fuck about what Ichabod Crane had to say. And yet, she couldn't stop thinking about him. Even though years have passed, she still feels affected by his presence. Her friend Analyn loved to brag about her son at every opportunity. Despite time passing, Drusilla was still haunted by her feelings for him. Ichabod Crane had been her best friend, and he had been the only person who saw her for who she was and not just as Katrina's weird, nerdy older sister.

Focus, Drusilla chided herself and got back to work.

She double-checked her findings so far and frowned at the body. To her frustration, Drusilla didn't find much of anything beyond what she'd already observed during her preliminary examination at the crime scene. She swabbed Carter's hands and severed head. She took the typical blood and urine samples and sent them to the lab upstairs.

Drusilla sighed and pulled off her gloves and apron before throwing them in a secure disposal container. She wheeled the body to the wall of refrigerated lockers and opened the drawer to slide Carter's body inside.

After storing the corpse, Drusilla walked over to her desk, which was tucked into a corner of the morgue, and started her initial report to Dr. Willard. There wasn't enough sad coffee sludge in the world to make her want to tell Dr. Willard that she had nothing until the lab results came in, but she did it anyway.

Unless the results said otherwise, Denis Carter had died of acute, sharp force trauma to the head.

Beyond that, all she could do was hope that she would get authorization from Dr. Salazar to do a full internal autopsy.

She had just been pressing send on her report when the doors to the morgue opened and Kyndall walked in. Her assistant swapped her scrubs for a t-shirt and jeans that revealed her stunning muscular body. Kyndall was thick with sepia-colored skin and long, platinum box braids that fell down her back, while Drusilla was built flatter than a plank of wood.

She suddenly remembered all the reasons why she had ended up in Kyndall's bed. Their brief affair had been intense and passionate. Although they had great sexual chemistry, both women decided to remain friends.

"Time to clock out," Kyndall said, crossing her arms.

"I still got too much work to do," Drusilla protested. "The paperwork's not going to do itself."

Kyndall snorted, then walked over and closed the lid of Drusilla's laptop.

Drusilla glared at her. "Now I know you're trippin'"

"The only one trippin' here is you." Kyndall rolled her eyes. "Take yo' ass home and go to sleep."

Drusilla opened her mouth to argue, but Kyndall wasn't going to take no for an answer. She sighed as Kyndall tugged her up onto her feet.

"Now, I will be magnanimous and lock up for you," Kyndall said.

"I'm your boss," Drusilla weakly complained as she gathered her things. "You're supposed to listen to me."

"Uh-huh." Kyndall rolled her eyes as she turned off the lights.

Drusilla walked out through the double doors, wondering why she thought hiring her best friend had been a good idea.

Four

Unspoken Rules

Drusilla knew she should just go home, but instead of making a beeline for her nice, comfortable bed, she headed back down the Cross-Westchester Expressway and into Sleepy Hollow.

Ten minutes later, she turned the corner onto Hemlock Drive. Despite the ominous name, the street was a perfect example of upper-middle-class suburbia. Picturesque two-story colonial homes and green, neatly manicured lawns were slightly hidden behind sharply clipped hedge bushes.

It was like driving down the set of a fifties sitcom.

The neighborhood was on the other side of the preserve and a little too close to the historic Philipsburg Manor. It was the pride and joy of Sleepy Hollow, but the place was no better than a plantation, and her Black ass hated even driving past the place. Her sister, on the other hand, thought that Drusilla was being too dramatic.

She pulled up in front of her sister's two-story Dutch colonial. The top floor was white, and the bottom was a brown brick. Light gray shutters framed the windows, and two columns framed a black door. It was perfectly boring and nothing like the manor where they'd both grown up: a dark, menacing thing that seemed to loom over any structure in a fifty-mile radius. Grimwood, that 18th-century Victorian estate, had been built after a fire destroyed the original Van Tassel homestead in 1793.

The name–Grimwood–had been ironic when the place had been painted a cheery, pale yellow, but now it fits the name perfectly with its pitch-black exterior.

"Stop stalling, Drusilla," she muttered to herself.

Honestly, she didn't want to go in there. Drusilla knew that her sister wouldn't be happy to see her. But she had to put her big girl panties on. With a sigh, Drusilla got out of the car and trudged up the brick path that led to the door.

She knocked but there was nothing.

Drusilla knocked repeatedly and still got no answer.

"Katrina!" Drusilla banged on the door. "I know you're in there. Open the goddamn door."

Her sister finally opened up and glared at Drusilla. "Stop making a scene!" Katrina hissed venomously.

Then, as if on cue, she plastered on her practiced toothpaste commercial smile and waved at someone behind Drusilla.

Drusilla turned to see an elderly white woman kneeling in her garden with a huge wide-brim hat and a pair of garden shears in her hand staring right at them. Another perk of living at the manor: no nosy neighbors.

And, no, Hobbs didn't count.

Katrina pulled her into the house and slammed the door. She huffed and then brushed non-existent dust off of a white and black polka-dotted blouse. She wore a yellow, pleated A-line skirt and her black patent leather Jimmy Choo pumps. Despite retiring from modeling, Katrina still looked like she belonged on the pages of a magazine. Meanwhile, Drusilla looked like a hot mess dressed in scrubs and her Chucks with her hair still done up in twists.

Despite being twins, the only things they shared in appearance were their dark round-shaped eyes, button noses, and full lips. Katrina was a few shades lighter than Drusilla's umber-colored skin. Drusilla's natural hair stayed in a twist-out, while Katrina's hair had been dyed a chestnut brown and laid within an inch of its life. And unlike Drusilla, Katrina was tall and willowy, which was perfect for the catwalks she used to dominate.

With a sigh, Drusilla shoved her way past Katrina and sat down on the dark tan recliner.

"No." Katrina marched over and jerked her out of the chair. "Anywhere but there."

Drusilla just stared at her sister and then down at the chair. 'What the hell?'

Then she remembered this had been Brom's favorite chair. It had been so long since she'd visited her sister that she'd forgotten the chair was off-limits. She suddenly felt sick and scrambled over to the white sofa.

"Why are you even here?" Katrina glared down at her.

"I just wanted to see if you were alright."

Drusilla perched tentatively at the end of the couch, her eyes darting back to the chair and then to the wall full of framed photos. All of them were of Katrina and Brom. Every image on the wall represented a memory, starting from childhood, when Brom had been a cute, little white boy with a smile that often got him what he wanted-which included always having Katrina by his side. Even back then, she only had eyes for him.

The photos progressed from elementary to middle to high school. There was one where Brom was still in his football uniform, and in his arms with her head thrown back in a laugh was Katrina in her orange and black cheerleading uniform. At center stage was a photo from their wedding. Katrina and Brom were pressed together as they looked into each other's eyes.

"I'm fine. And if that's all you wanted, then you can go," Katrina said, flipping her hair.

Drusilla moved uncomfortably in her seat and then frowned when her foot hit something. Bending down, she picked it up. Clutching the book to her, Drusilla shot a glare at her sister. This book was the family bible. Within, there was a comprehensive list of all the births and deaths in the Van Tassel family since before they arrived from the Netherlands in 1741.

Despite their father having split his estate evenly between the two sisters. Katrina was made wealthy by Brom's life insurance and had no interest in Grimwood. The only thing Katrina wanted was the family bible.

Drusilla wasn't religious and if the bible gave Katrina comfort? Then how could she say no? Back then, Drusilla reluctantly handed it over and now she found it being treated like some cheap paperback.

Katrina's eyes widened as she snatched it back. "I have no idea how it ended up there."

"Katrina, that thing is an antique. If you don't want it—"

Spinning around, Katrina scowled at Drusilla, "You're not my father, so don't lecture me. "

Katrina never responded well to their father's lectures. Nothing was more punishing for Drusilla than failing to meet her father's expectations. She would just sit there and receive the lectures in silence. Conversely, Katrina never gave in, which led to loud and fiery confrontations with their father.

With a sigh, Drusilla pinched the bridge of her nose. Katrina's mishandling of the bible upset her, but she understood it was a tough time for Katrina. Another person close to her has just died. "Look, I didn't come here to argue with you. I am sure you have heard about Denis."

"Yes, Ichabod was eager to tell me when I saw him earlier," Katrina bit out, "He is annoying as ever"

Drusilla froze, feeling sick to her stomach, "Ichabod was here?"

Katrina gave a disapproving stare, " Yes, he dropped by an hour ago." "Please tell me you still don't have feelings for that loser."

"No!", Drusilla shook her head, "Absolutely not!"

"Anyways," Katrina rolled her eyes. "I have a meeting with Pastor Sparks in fifteen minutes."

"I'm sorry about Denis," Drusilla said. "I knew how close you were to him."

Drusilla could see that, beyond Katrina's usual scorn, there was something broken and heart-achingly vulnerable in her twin's eyes. Katrina and Drusilla had never been close, but you don't live in the same household for eighteen years and not learn how to see through each other's masks. Unfortunately, that also meant that Katrina had a habit of sucker-punching Drusilla at her weakest points.

Katrina spun around and marched into the kitchen. "Do you want coffee? I could really go for a coffee right now."

Drusilla stood up, quickly rounded the coffee table, and wrapped her arms around her younger sister (by three minutes, so Drusilla counted as the older of the two). Katrina stood rigidly in her arms for a long moment. She really thought that Katrina would push her away like she always did, but to Drusilla's amazement, Katrina slumped in her arms and tentatively hugged her back.

It seemed like Drusilla held onto her sister forever. As they clung to each other, Drusilla wished that things had been different between them. There were so many things she wanted to tell

Katrina: that she loved her, that she wasn't alone in her grief, that no matter what happened, and no matter how much Katrina pushed her away, Drusilla would always be there.

Yet, no matter how hard she tried, the words wouldn't come.

Finally, Katrina backed away, and Drusilla let her arms drop limply to her side. She stared at her sister as she took a handkerchief from her pocket and dabbed her eyes, careful to make sure that none of her mascara ran.

"I'm going over to see Saundra," Katrina said, turning to finally meet Drusilla's eyes.

"What happened was—" Drusilla stopped, not knowing what to say. Finally, she settled on, "A lot. Saundra didn't take it well."

Katrina's gaze travailed to her wedding photo, her mouth pinched in a firm line. "Losing your husband can do that to you." Her voice was soft, her eyes distant.

"Katrina—" Drusilla started to say, but their shared moment was over, and the haughty mask that her sister often wore settled back into place.

This was Katrina Van Brunt: homecoming queen, head cheerleader, Miss Sleepy Hollow, and the woman who reigned over the town's wealthy elite with an iron fist. This Katrina had little time for her socially awkward big sister, and while they might only be a few feet apart, the chasm between them seemed impossible to cross.

This is the woman that Ichabod loved. She thought about the confrontation she had with her ex-best friend earlier. He was too quick to bring up Katrina. Back in the day, He used to follow

Katrina around like a lost puppy. Ichabod was no longer a lanky, awkward teenager. With her sister, this version of him might be more successful.

"Ridiculous," Drusilla muttered to herself. Katrina's longing for Brom never faded, even after his death.

Drusilla shoved that thought back into the mental box where she kept all of her inconvenient feelings.

"Pastor Sparks and I are going to meet up at Saundra's sister's house," Katrina said. "We want to support Saundra as much as we can right now."

"That's nice of you," Drusilla grimaced.

Her stomach was tied up in knots. Her mind went back to the crime scene this morning. Drusilla could still hear Saundra's screams.

"And with Thornton being an incompetent buffoon," Katrina continued, "this is going to be Saundra's first day on a very long and tiring journey."

"Kat, Brom was..." Drusilla sighed and closed her eyes.

Did she want to get into this old argument again? It had been a year since Brom's body had been found in the middle of the preserve. Dr. Willard had been in charge of that case and determined it to be a suicide. Dr. Willard was an asshole, but he was also one of the best forensic pathologists in the state. Thornton had had no reason to doubt the autopsy's findings.

"No, I don't want to hear it," Katrina replied, looking away. "You're just like everyone else. I'm not crazy!"

"You're not crazy." Drusilla put her hands up, "But I don't want to argue with you."

Katrina didn't say anything. Her complete attention was on her wedding photo. Drusilla bit her lip. After Brom's death, Katrina went off the deep end. She was insistent that Brom had been murdered. She fought the Sheriff, the Mayor, and, hell, even Brom's own family to get his case reopened.

Rumors about Katrina's mental illness quickly spread around town. It took some weeks for Katrina to pull both herself and her reputation out of the mud. Since then, she'd slapped on the persona of a socialite and selfless philanthropist, and it had only gotten worse since their father's death.

It bothered her that Katrina would visit Brom's grave but refuse to visit their father's. Baltus's final resting place was tended to solely by Drusilla, who swept the dirt and fallen leaves and added fresh flowers every week. Katrina seemed to have no love to spare her family, despite their father being their sole parent since they were six.

Yet for the first time since Brom's death, Drusilla can get a peek at her twin's vulnerable pieces.

"My Brom was lying in that godforsaken preserve for hours while the sheriff was probably sitting on his ass at the donut shop," Katrina said softly to herself. She drifted her fingers along the glass covering her wedding photo, as if she wanted to teleport herself inside to a happier time.

Drusilla knew right then and there was nothing she could say to her sister that would make her change her mind. Katrina had made up her mind a long time ago, and as Drusilla stood there, she felt the emotional breach between them widen that much further.

Drusilla could only stand there and take it. She clenched her fists, her eyes stinging with unshed tears.

"I'll go." Drusilla stood up and walked over to her sister.

Katrina didn't turn to look at her. Drusilla raised her hand, her fingers hovering over Katrina's stiff shoulders, but with a defeated sigh, she slowly lowered them. Drusilla turned and walked out the door.

Five

No Room For Error

Drusilla woke up from the nightmare again a few days after Denis' body was discovered. The veil between reality and the horrifying dream was thin, and it took her a few moments to remember who she was. She wasn't Mathilde, escaping from the Horseman's deadly clutches.

She closed her eyes as the alarm on her phone went off. She turned it off and sat up in bed. As she swiped through the missed texts, she saw there was nothing from Katrina–and no missed calls, either. Drusilla groaned and put her head in her hands.

The silence between her and her sister had promptly resumed after their conversation the other day. Drusilla had given her sister a few days to cool down in some futile hope that Katrina would see reason, but she should've known better. As the days passed, Katrina's silence filled Drusilla with unease.

A wall stood between them, solid and immovable. She feared that Denis' murder and the aftermath of it would be the final brick in that wall, the one that meant it could never be torn down.

Drusilla quickly got dressed in a green, oversized cable-knit sweater and jeans and headed downstairs. She paused in front of the horn and patted it.

"I think I really screwed up this time, Dad," she murmured to the horn before stepping out the door.

As Drusilla waved goodbye to Hobbs and the other farmhands, she tried her best to bury her feelings by thinking about work. She had finished her examination of Denis' body and was waiting on the lab results before she sent off the final report to Dr. Willard and Sheriff Thornton. She'd tried her best to distract herself in the meantime by concentrating on her massive backlog. Being a medical examiner didn't always mean dramatic beheadings. There had been a tragic accident on Saw Mill River Parkway, a man who'd died suddenly in his sleep, and a poor woman who had been fished out of the Tappan Zee.

Drusilla drove past Broadway, which was the center of the small town, and she was surprised to see Ichabod Crane walking out of Davidson's Ballistics, a gun store popular with the hunters who came to the area during deer and turkey season. Ichabod Crane had always snubbed his aquiline nose at the hunters. So it was odd that the same man who had adamantly refused to go to the range with her was now walking out of a gun store.

Growing up in Sleepy Hollow, she'd long since learned that guns and hunting were just part of the culture. Her father had been an avid hunter himself and had no qualms about teaching his daughters how to shoot. Like everything else, Katrina was an excellent marksman. Drusilla was much better with a compound bow, but she hated to hunt, though not as much as Ichabod.

The man seemed to haunt her with every step. In her brief moments of freedom, Drusilla kept running into him all over town. She saw him in line at her one of favorite lunch spots, in the library, bent over a laptop, with his eyes completely focused on the screen. She caught sight of him jogging down the trail in Devries Park.

Drusilla jumped as she heard a loud horn and some cursing. She felt her cheeks flush and waved apologetically as she drove away. Yet, as she made her way to work, Try as she might, Drusilla couldn't stop her thoughts from circling back to Ichabod.

Has he changed so much?

It had been sixteen years, and god knew that Drusilla wasn't the same person she'd once been. However, no matter how much she tried to deny it, it disconcerted her that this Ichabod had been nothing more than a stranger with a familiar face.

Drusilla entered the morgue and noticed that she was alone. None of her assistants were there yet. She checked the time on her phone and saw that she was fifteen minutes early to work. With a sigh, Drusilla walked over to her desk. She quickly started up her computer, winced at the amount of emails, and then knocked back the last of her coffee.

There were requests for statements from various news organizations, and Drusilla sighed when she spotted an email from Estelle Cruz. Drusilla deleted Estelle's email and all the other interview requests and was just starting to look through the interdepartmental emails when Kyndall walked through the door with a strange look on her face.

"What?"

"Willard wants to see you."

"Great," Drusilla groaned. "Just great."

"It's probably just to bust your ass about the paperwork."

Drusilla grimaced and stood. "Wish me luck."

Kyndall patted her sympathetically on the shoulder. "Good luck."

Drusilla made her way out of the morgue and down the long hallway, passing a few empty stretchers to the elevator. Though she didn't hurry, it took her no time at all to arrive at Dr. Willard's office on the top floor.

His assistant, a perky white woman who looked only a few years younger than Drusilla, distractedly waved her in. Drusilla knocked on the door.

"Come in."

Drusilla took a deep breath and proceeded into the large office. "You wanted to see me, Dr. Willard?"

Dr. Willard looked up from the file and waved her to the chair in front of his large, dark-wood desk. "I wanted to talk to you about the Carter case."

He was a thin white man and had a gaunt face and short, thinning hair that had gone gray with age. His dark brown eyes peered down at her behind the narrow, square-rimmed glasses perched on his nose.

Dr. Willard tapped his thin, bony fingers on the desk. "This report is very concise."

Drusilla plastered on a smile. "It was a straightforward case of acute sharp force trauma. I can't make a final determination without the toxicology results and the report from forensics."

Dr. Willard reached over the inbox tray and picked up another folder, opening it and scanning the contents. "Lucky for you, then, since the reports just came in today."

Drusilla straightened up, her eyes going wide. There'd been nothing in her email about this. Why had the lab gone over her head and sent it to Dr. Willard first?

They don't trust me, Drusilla thought.

She gritted her teeth. She'd been a full-time medical examiner here for six months and had worked part-time for over a year before that. Not to mention all the years she worked at the city's Medical Examiner's office. She had hoped that the quality of her work would speak for itself.

Another part of her, the cool, logical person Drusilla had painstakingly cultivated, told her she was being completely absurd. This was a big case. Denis was a *Carter*. The Carters were an old influential family. Of course, they would go directly to Willard. It was an important case.

It still didn't sit quite right in her spirit.

Drusilla took a deep breath and tried to push away her unease as she scanned the reports. No traces of drugs or poisons and only minute traces of alcohol.

"It was an ax." Drusilla had suspected as much right from the jump, but just as she'd told Thornton, she hadn't wanted to make assumptions.

"Yes." Dr. Willard leaned forward. "Forensics ran a carbon analysis on some shards of the handle that were found on the body. It dates back to the late 18th century."

Drusilla could only stare at her supervisor in bewilderment. There was someone actually going around and whacking people's heads off with an antique from the *Revolutionary War*. Her mind went back to her nightmares and the way the Horseman's head had fallen to the ground.

Stop it, Drusilla chided herself.

The tale of the Horseman was just a story to scare children. It wasn't real. This was undoubtedly the work of a disturbed person who had an infatuation with using an ancient relic to commit murder.

"It is strange." Dr. Willard shook his head. "I know that people here are heavily invested in Revolutionary history; I've witnessed quite a few war reenactments since I moved here. But to kill someone with an 18th-century ax is bizarre."

Drusilla silently agreed. Sleepy Hollow was proud of their history and the town's contribution to the Revolutionary War. It came with living in the Hudson River Valley, where most of the battles took place. Fort Stanwix was only an hour and a half away from Sleepy Hollow, and the Battle of Oriskany wasn't the only famous battle from the revolution that had occurred near here.

"Sadly, this isn't the strangest case I've taken on," Drusilla said.

"Yes, I gather you saw your fair share of strange cases working for the city." Dr. Willard drummed his fingers on his desk, "Nevertheless, it's important that we solve this case as quickly as possible."

"I understand, sir."

"I want you to re-examine the body," He ordered. "With this much scrutiny, there's no room for error."

Drusilla inwardly sighed. She should've been expecting this. She could tell her supervisor that she'd already been over it twice since she took custody of Carter's body, but she knew he'd just ask her to triple-check it.

In the end, Drusilla took a deep breath and simply replied, "Of course, sir."

Dr. Willard nodded and turned back to the paperwork. With that clear dismissal, Drusilla clutched the report to her chest and marched out of his office, then hurried down the hallway and onto the balcony that looked into the bustling lobby.

With the booming crime rate, Westchester County had taken the initiative to condense the forensics and coroner's offices into one building. Drusilla didn't think that it was a good idea. It crossed the unspoken lines of forensics. The lab geeks steered clear of the basement dwellers, and the feeling was entirely mutual.

She went down the stairs, through the sleek, modern lobby, and to the elevators. People gave her a wide berth; she could hear them whispering as she passed. Drusilla did her best to ignore them as much as she could. Yet, she couldn't deny that the constant scrutiny was beginning to get to her. She gave a sigh of relief as she finally got inside the elevators and clicked the button that would take her to the basement.

It seemed like everyone wanted a piece of her lately, and Drusilla was sick of it. She was used to being in the background. Yet, now she found herself center stage. It reminded her of Ichabod and his utter audacity in asking her for confidential information. When he mentioned Katrina, there was a certain look in his eyes. Drusilla could have sworn she saw a hint of longing there. *But maybe I'm just imagining it?* Drusilla knew she was heavily biased when it came to Ichabod.

She inwardly sighed, *It is such a goddamn shame that he is such an insufferable asshole.* The man was fine as hell and it had been a while since any man had caught her attention, and it was just her luck that the first man to truly captivate her in years was Ichabod Crane, of all people.

"I need to get my shit together," Drusilla sighed to herself as she stepped off the elevator and headed back to work.

Six

Irreconcilable Differences

Drusilla frowned at Denis' body, which was laid out on the cool slab. She redid the external examination. She x-rayed the body, checked Denis's teeth against his dental records, and re-examined the detached head. Additionally, she took samples from Denis's mouth and ears and the ragged cut in his neck. Diligently, she checked over his feet and fingernails for trace evidence.

Drusilla picked up her scalpel and made a Y-incision, exposing Denis's heart and lungs. *I never thought I would see you like this,*

Drusilla thought to herself as she took another blood sample. In the end, the result was the same.

Drusilla growled in frustration as she ripped off her gloves and apron and threw them into the secure disposal unit. The manner of death for Denis Carter was still acute sharp force trauma to the neck. Drusilla had just wasted her time doing a full autopsy.

"Nothing," She said, disgusted as she jerked the surgical mask off and threw it away.

Kyndall shook her head. "What did Willard expect for you to find? A map that'll lead you straight to Carter's murderer?"

"Apparently." Drusilla threw up her hands. "But I can't make evidence magically appear."

"Yeah, but they still want you to play whipping girl." Kyndall snorted in clear disgust. "Maybe if they stopped expecting you to do their job for them, we could get somewhere."

"Preach," Drusilla said, shaking her head.

Her phone rang, and Drusilla walked over to her desk. She was hoping it was Katrina but frowned when she saw the display.

"Hello, Áte," Drusilla answered, her cheeks flushing red.

"Hello, Drusilla." It was Analyn Crane. Her soft voice was a lilting mixture of British and her native Tagalong. Ichabod's mixed nationality and ethnicity were reflected in his character. Not unlike his British Filipino mother, he had dual citizenship in both the United States and The United Kingdom. His white American father had grown up in Sleepy Hollow and had brought Ichabod kicking and screaming to the States when he was Fifteen.

"I'm sorry I haven't called you in a while," Drusilla rushed to apologize. "It's been crazy at work."

"This time of year brings all the weirdos out," Analyn said. "I do hope you are being careful."

Drusilla sighed. "As I can be."

"Well, I won't keep you long. Ichabod has finally come home."

"I know! "I saw him a few days ago," Drusilla said with feigned enthusiasm.

She loved Analyn, but god, the last thing Drusilla wanted to do was spend an hour on the phone as she gushed over her prodigal son.

"I didn't think he would ever come home.," Analyn replied excitedly.

I wish he never did, Drusilla thought to herself, then winced.

That wasn't fair to Analyn. She sounded absolutely ecstatic. No matter how close Drusilla and Analyn were, Ichabod was still her son.

And Drusilla was still just an orphan Analyn took pity on.

"Well, I wanted to invite you to dinner this Friday. I know Ichabod would love to see you."

Drusilla barely repressed a snort because she'd seen quite enough of him as it was. She didn't want to be trapped in a homecoming party. Analyn was open about her wish for Ichabod to return, settle down with Drusilla, and give her grandchildren. Her friend's mention of Ichabod hurt her every time, but she kept it to herself.

The happy homemaker lifestyle did not appeal to Drusilla as it did to Katrina. Deep down, Drusilla had always dreamed that Ichabod would choose her and they would have a happily ever after of their own. Despite trying to move on for the last sixteen years, Drusilla couldn't help but compare all of her partners to Ichabod and the illusion of closeness they once shared.

"Drusilla?" Analyn asked, breaking Drusilla out of her thoughts. "Are you there?"

"I'm here!"

"That's great! I was worried the call dropped." Analyn giggled. "Did I tell you I was making puto?"

Drusilla bit back a groan. Puto was steamed rice cakes that were not only delicious but addictive. She could almost taste the rice, sugar, and coconut on her tongue. "Oh, you're playing dirty."

Analyn only chuckled, and Drusilla felt her mouth ticking into a small reluctant smile.

"I have to work that night." Drusilla had never been more grateful for her busy work schedule.

"Can't you just come for an hour or two before your shift?"

Absolutely not! she thought. But out loud, she said, "Okay."

Drusilla slapped her forehead and wanted to immediately take it back.

"That's great!" Analyn gushed. "I'll see you Friday around eight?"

Drusilla reluctantly agreed but wanted to knock her head against her desk. Instead of avoiding Ichabod Crane, Drusilla had just agreed to go to that bastard's homecoming party. What was her fucking life?

"What the hell am I doing?" Drusilla muttered to herself as she stood just outside Analyn's front door. The entire rest of the week, Drusilla had been devising increasingly ridiculous plans to skip the dinner. Here she was, waiting to subject herself to this farce.

She raised her hand to knock and then stopped herself. Drusilla could turn around and leave, and say something had come up. But did she want to do that to Analyn?

She fidgeted with the end of her short skirt, something she normally wouldn't have worn. She much preferred scrubs or her cozy, oversized sweaters and jeans. The skirt had been a gift. "Maybe if you stopped dressing like a grandma, you could get a date," Katrina had told her as she'd shoved the skirt into her hand last Christmas.

And while Drusilla didn't want a date with Ichabod, she could at least show him what he'd missed out on after he left. According to some, the first love always leaves the deepest wound. That had definitely been the case for her. No matter how hard she tried, the void created by Ichabod's disappearance remained unfilled.

I need to go back to therapy.

Drusilla went to knock again but stopped herself. *This is such a bad idea.*

Her stomach twisted into knots. But suddenly, Drusilla felt a pair of eyes boring into her back. Freezing, she slowly turned around to see Ichabod standing at the end of the short hallway. His gaze raked boldly over her.

Drusilla shivered, once again debating the logic of her outfit. She wore a tight, black turtleneck, way-too-short burnt orange corduroy skirt, black wool tights, and four-inch calf-height charcoal-colored boots.

"You are such a creeper," she scolded.

Ichabod walked down the hallway, his long strides strangely graceful. Back in the day, he'd been clumsy, constantly tripping over his own feet. Drusilla wished for a trip now. Crashing face first to the ground would certainly wipe that smug look off his face.

"I was waiting for you to figure out if you were going to knock on the door or leave. My money is on the latter." Ichabod shrugged. "You always loved running away from your problems."

Drusilla stepped forward, "You got a lot of nerve. Last time I checked, I wasn't the one who refused to step foot in the Hollow for sixteen years. If anyone's the coward here, Ichabod Crane, it's you."

Drusilla turned to knock on the door, but Ichabod grabbed her and spun her around. He was in her personal space now, their faces inches away from her.

Close enough to kiss, Drusilla thought to herself, but this wasn't the time to be thirsty.

Ichabod stared down at her, his hazel eyes burning hot with anger and hurt. "You were the one who ghosted me without saying a word."

"Yeah with damn good reason," she snarled. "You were the one that—"

The door opened, and they both turned to see Analyn Crane standing in the doorway.

"You don't waste any time, son."

"Nanay!" Ichabod jerked away, and ironically, it was Drusilla who almost tripped.

"Come on in, both of you." Analyn waved them inside. "Dinner's almost ready."

Ichabod sighed and then hurried inside, only stopping to give his mother a quick peck on her cheek as he passed. Awkwardly, Drusilla walked into the apartment.

Analyn's dark brown eyes twinkled in mirth. "I told you Ichabod would love to see you."

Drusilla felt her cheeks flush in embarrassment but thought the best thing for her was to just change the subject. "You look wonderful, Áte. Are you sure that I'm not underdressed?"

"You look wonderful, darling."

Drusilla bit her lip as she took in Analyn's outfit. The older woman was resplendent in a vintage Dior black a-line dress, and the diamonds around her neck contrasted nicely against her golden brown skin. Drusilla noticed that her dark brown hair had been cut into a short, stylish bob. Even hitting sixty, the only sign of Analyn's age was the streaks of gray in her hair.

"You look beautiful," Analyn reassured her as she kissed Drusilla on the cheek. "My son certainly thinks so."

"Analyn!" Drusilla hissed, feeling her cheeks heat even more.

Analyn chuckled. "It's true. But I'll leave it be. Come along before dinner gets cold."

Drusilla followed her further into the condo, and immediately, her nose was filled with the mouthwatering smells of food. Her stomach rumbled in protest as the delicious aromas of spices hit.

Drusilla sighed as she walked through the condo. The place was huge, with an open layout, and just as opulent as its owner. A dove-gray sectional took up most of the living room, and next to it was a round coffee table and a side table. Dominating the floor underfoot was a massive, cobalt-blue Persian rug that probably cost more than her monthly salary. The lights of the lighthouse filtered through two tall windows that looked out onto the Hudson River.

Drusilla walked past the sofa and made her way to the large dining room with its cherry wood dining table. In the center was a beautiful candelabra and a centerpiece of peonies. Analyn's table had beautiful place settings of blue china sitting on top of silver chargers. It wasn't the usual plates that she used whenever

Drusilla came over. No, these were her prized white-and-blue floral dishes that typically sat untouched in the hutch.

Analyn must be pulling out all the stops for this dinner, Drusilla thought to herself as both women sat down at the table.

Analyn sat at the head, with Drusilla on her right. Ichabod came out of the kitchen carrying a tray of food and set it down on the table. Besides the main course of pork adobo he'd just brought out, she spotted pata hamonado, skinless longanisa, and beef empanadas. No sight of the rice cakes that had lured her there, though.

"This all looks so amazing, thank you," Drusilla told Analyn.

"You're welcome, darling." Analyn smiled, "You know I only cook for the people I love."

A warmth bloomed in Drusilla's chest as she thought of the many times the older woman had cooked for her in the past.

Analyn turned to give her son a fond smile. He returned it, and the man was so damn gorgeous when he smiled.

"Thank you, Nanay," he said. "I'm sorry; I shouldn't have stayed away for so long."

Drusilla abruptly looked away, feeling suddenly like an intruder in a private moment.

Analyn's gaze softened, and she leaned over to squeeze his hand. "It's alright. After your father—" Analyn stopped and looked away. "It's understandable."

Drusilla finally looked over at Ichabod. His mouth was pinched in a firm line as he clutched his fork. He'd always been an arrogant know-it-all, but before Lt. General Crane had died, Ichabod had been softer and more open. After his father's death, he'd become someone harder and crueler.

She hadn't understood back then how grief could change a person, but Drusilla knew firsthand with Katrina's obsession over Brom's death and then the slow decline of her father.

A month after Drusilla broke off their friendship, towards the end of their senior year. Ichabod and his father had been in a horrific car accident, and he had been the lone survivor. The accident didn't leave him with many injuries, but it was obvious that Ichabod blamed himself.

Ichabod had practically ripped out her heart and stomped on it. But even as angry as Drusilla had been (and still was) she never wished that type of pain on him.

"I don't need your pity," Ichabod had sneered at her at his father's funeral after she'd told him how sorry she was for his loss.

His face had been twisted into a mask of rage and grief. Even after all Ichabod had done to her, Drusilla had still come to comfort him, and he'd thrown that back in her face.

Two weeks later, Graduation happened and Ichabod simply faded from her life.

Analyn coughed and forced a smile. "Now, enough of the heavy stuff." She waved it off. "Did I tell you Ichabod got a job at Diedrich?"

"It's temporary," Ichabod said dismissively. "It's only an adjunct position."

"Oh, hush. You getting a job at one of the most prestigious universities in the state is nothing to sniff at."

"You must be proud," Drusilla said, after taking a bite into the longanisa.

"I am. I bet if he works hard, then he might get offered a permanent position." Analyn gave Ichabod a proud smile.

Ichabod winced and hastily swallowed his food. "Let's not get our hopes up. With this recession, I would be surprised if I'm even up for consideration."

Analyn rolled her eyes and turned to Drusilla. "He's so humble."

Drusilla just barely stopped herself from snorting and popped a bit of pork into her mouth to keep from answering. Then, a phone rang. Thankfully, it wasn't her ringtone. She hated being called into work early.

Ichabod, however, threw his mother a sheepish look and pulled out his phone. He looked at the display and sighed. "Sorry, Nanay. I got to take this."

Analyn threw her son a disapproving glare. "Ichabod Benigno Crane—"

Ichabod kissed his mother on the cheek and hurried away.

She huffed. "That boy. He's always running off."

Drusilla bit her lip, but she could only silently agree. Not that she cared about what Ichabod did with his time, but he'd been running since his father's death. He traveled around the world, never staying in one place too long. The wanderlust might be due to Ichabod's ADHD, but Drusilla suspected there was more to it.

Eventually, Ichabod returned, a deep frown on his face.

"What is it?" his mother asked.

He shook his head. "There is an emergency at work."

Drusilla frowned, "Aren't you a professor? What kind of work emergency could you possibly have right now?"

Ichabod rolled his eyes. "Like most people these days, I have a second job. Can't pay the bills on a teacher's salary anymore."

"Do you have to go?" Analyn asked. "Can't they find someone else?"

"Afraid not, Nanay." Ichabod kissed her on the cheek.

"Be careful, Ichabod." Analyn patted his cheek in return. "A murderer is running around."

Ichabod reassured his mother that he would be alright and threw a strange, fleeting gaze at Drusilla before leaving.

Seven

The Edge of Danger

Later that night, Drusilla drove down the long, narrow country road leading to the expressway. It was a back road, but it was Friday night, and downtown was packed full of people looking for a good time. She wouldn't have taken this road at all, but Drusilla spent longer than she should have at Analyn's condo, and she couldn't be late for work.

Drusilla yawned and turned up the radio. The night was dark enough that all she could see was the outline of the trees swaying back and forth in the frigid autumn wind. The only light was the full moon peeking through the tall branches.

As she drove, she thought about the interesting evening she'd just had. After her son left, Analyn pasted on a cheery smile and tried to pretend that she was okay. But Ichabod's abrupt disappearance had clearly hurt her. She had spent all that time fixing his favorite meal, only for him to ditch her.

Drusilla tapped her fingers along with Haunted by Poe. The song's melancholy lyrics made her think of Ichabod. She couldn't help but wonder about Ichabod's second job and his sudden work emergency. It would be just like him to have made it up in order to leave early.

She caught sight of a blur of movement from the corner of her eye and then something darted in front of her car. Drusilla slammed her foot down on the brakes, making her car come to a screeching halt.

Only inches away from her was a white woman in a torn dress, her long, blonde hair matted and her eyes wide with fear.

"Saundra?" Drusilla recognized the woman instantly got out of the car and ran over to her.

Saundra Carter looked up, her eyes terrified, and took a step back. "Dr-Drusilla?"

"What happened?" Drusilla demanded. "Who did this to you?"

Saundra's typical contempt for her was absent, replaced by a frantic desperation, "Please help me!"

"Come on, I'll take you to the hospital."

The strength of Saundra's grip bit into her arm, her nails digging into Drusilla's skin. "You have to help me!"

"I'm trying," Drusilla pleaded. "Just let me just get you in the car."

She pushed her towards the car, but suddenly, the sound of clomping hooves rang out through the night air, and Saundra shook.

"Oh god, it's him!" the other woman sobbed.

Drusilla ran to the car, practically dragging a struggling Saundra over to the passenger seat, and shoved the woman inside. Then she dashed to the driver's side, slamming her door closed when she spotted a shadow in the trees. It was clearly an enormous man on horseback, just out of reach of the Lincoln's high beams. In the moonlight, she could make out the absence of a head and the ax in his hands.

Her own hands shaking, Drusilla put the keys in the ignition, but the engine spluttered and went dead.

"Shit!" Drusilla slammed her hands on the steering wheel.

"W-we're going to die, aren't we?" Saundra stuttered.

"No, the fuck we're not!"

A piercing, high-pitched screech made Drusilla jump. Then suddenly, the passenger's side door was ripped off its hinges. Drusilla screamed as Saundra was jerked out of the car. She snatched her phone and scrambled after the poor woman just in time for an ax to fall. Saundra's head tumbled off her shoulders onto the ground. Her body slumped forward as blood pooled around her.

Time appeared to slow down for Drusilla as she turned and came face to face with the manifestation of her worst nightmare.

The Horseman stood eerily still beside Saundra's headless corpse. Its two-headed battle ax glimmered in the moonlight. A few feet away, Drusilla spotted the Horseman's white steed, patiently waiting for its master.

Drusilla bolted out of the car for the trees. *I just had to wear heels tonight,* Drusilla thought hysterically to herself as she darted through the forest. The tree branches tore at her skirt and scratched against her vulnerable skin. The forest was eerily silent, and she could only hear the beating of her own heart and the slap of her feet crunching through the fallen leaves. Drusilla knew if the Horseman discovered her, then she would be just as dead as Saundra.

Drusilla felt like her chest was going to collapse if she ran any farther. She stopped by a tree. Panting for breath, she clutched its hard bark for dear life. Her ears strained to hear the approach of the horseman.

There was only the unnatural stillness of the night.

Drusilla's fingers were shaking as she unlocked her phone.

"This is 911. What is your emergency?"

Drusilla froze as she heard the abrupt sounds of a horse approaching.

Her phone fell out of her slack fingers, and Drusilla turned and ran. The Horseman was on her heels, gaining on her with every passing second. And just like in her nightmares, he eventually caught up to her, yanking her up by her neck. His meaty hands bit into her skin, and she struggled to breathe as the Horseman lifted her with unnatural strength.

She stared wide-eyed at her attacker, desperately fighting against his hold, her fists futilely striking his muscular arm, but the Horseman did not budge. The ax rose in his other hand, glinting malevolently. *This was it. This was how I'm going to die.* In the split second before the ax met her exposed neck, A vision struck Drusilla, showing Mathilde in her position and the terror they felt.

An odd sensation rushed through her entire body; something hot as fire came up from her feet, through her legs and torso, and then out into her spread hands.

Though she didn't know why, Drusilla shouted, "Furche!"

Something sliced into the horsema's chest, as if done by an invisible knife.

Blood splattered onto her face, and she tasted cool copper on her tongue before falling to the ground. She coughed and wheezed for air, watching the Horseman jerk and convulse before dropping to the ground.

Drusilla shakily got to her feet and ran. Disoriented from the attack and hobbled by her damned heels, Drusilla tripped over a root and fell headfirst onto the forest floor, her fingers clawing at the fallen leaves and dirt.

Instinct had Drusilla twisting out of the way just in time to see an ax hit the dirt where her head had been seconds ago. Drusilla flipped onto her back and tried to scurry away as the Horseman picked up his ax and charged at her again.

That same fiery sensation from earlier seared through her, and a bright orange light poured out of her palm and through her fingers. The Horseman abruptly soared through the air and collided with a tree.

Drusilla stared at her glowing hands.

What is this? An anime? she thought hysterically to herself,

But she didn't have time to think about that because the Horseman was on his feet again. Before it could charge once more, Drusilla heard a loud bang. She ducked down and covered her ears, and the Horseman stumbled backward.

She watched in amazement as Ichabod walked out of the trees, holding a gun in his hands and shouting, "Stay away from her!"

Ichabod fired over and over again into the Horseman, but that didn't stop the terrifying figure, only slowed it down. But just as Ichabod finished firing the clip, the Horseman froze, awkwardly twitching and shaking before staggering back.

Pounding hooves thundered toward them, and she turned to see the horse galloping her way. She rolled out of the way so as not to get trampled, but the horse gave her a wide berth. To her amazement, the Horseman simply turned away from her, mounted his horse, and galloped away.

Eight

An Inkling Of The Truth

"Doctor?"

Drusilla snapped out of her reverie and looked at Deputy Hansen, who had been assigned to take her statement. Ichabod and Drusilla had trudged back to the road in stony silence and called the police. Now, she was stuck answering the same questions over and over when all she only wanted was a cup of coffee and a shower. She sighed and rubbed her pounding head.

"Sorry, can you repeat that?" she asked.

"Are you sure that you didn't get a good look at the perp?"

"No," Drusilla lied.

She felt a pang of guilt, but Drusilla knew that telling anyone about the Horseman would be a disaster, especially for her own sake. It would be the one excuse they needed to take her off this case. Besides, they already didn't take her seriously. They really would think she was crazy if her statement went anywhere near the truth.

Crazy.

Just like her sister.

Just like her mother.

The deputy sighed and put away his notebook. "Alright, you still need to come in for a formal statement, but for now, you can go."

Drusilla smiled, but it came out more like a grimace.

From somewhere nearby, she heard Ichabod shouted: "I was merely trying to help!"

Drusilla and Deputy Hansen turned to see Thornton giving Ichabod an unimpressed look. He looked like he was a father scolding a recalcitrant child. It was nice to see someone else get that treatment for once.

"You should have called the police and not tried to play the hero." Thornton shook his head. "We're keeping your gun for the time being, and we want you to come in tomorrow for a statement."

Ichabod huffed and crossed his arms. "Very well."

"Doc, you finished up here?" Thornton asked, walking over to her.

Drusilla nodded. "Yeah, I need to go to work, but—" She gestured to the mess that had once been her car.

"I can give her a ride home," Ichabod offered

Drusilla took a deep breath and then shook her head. The last thing she wanted was to be stuck in the car with Ichabod Crane. She was hesitant to accept a ride from the deputies, fearing an interrogation that might lead to her revealing inconvenient truths.

"I'm not going home," Drusilla stubbornly set her jaw. " I have work to do."

The two men exchanged concerned looks as she straightened to her full height–which wasn't much, compared to Sheriff Thornton and Ichabod–and threw them both a death glare.

"I don't think that is a good—" Thornton started.

Drusilla put her hand up to stop him. "I still have a job to do, and we need to stop this guy before he kills again."

Drusilla turned to Ichabod, who just stared blankly back at her. She barely stopped herself from rolling her eyes and marched over to the shiny gray Land Rover that had a white, purple, grey, and black demisexual flag sticker on the rear window. Drusilla didn't even need to ask if it was his car. The vehicle was just as pretentiously British as he was. Although surprised by Ichabod's apparent demisexuality, it was just one of many things she didn't know about this version of him.

Ichabod scrambled behind her. She paused in front of the door, then turned and lifted an eyebrow. "You going to unlock it for me?"

He sighed and silently used the remote to unlock the doors. Drusilla started to climb in when her foot slipped, but before she could fall, large, slim fingers wrapped around her waist. Drusilla gasped as Ichabod's body was a hot, hard line against her back.

"Alright there?" he said, and she barely bit back a whimper. Drusilla despised how effortlessly this man could shatter her mental walls with a mere touch.

His breath, smelling of peppermint, gently tickled her neck.

Drusilla coughed and shoved him away. "I'm fine."

She pulled herself into the cab and pointedly closed the door in his face. Drusilla regretted accepting his offer for a ride, but it was too late to ask Thornton for one. She waited impatiently for Ichabod to get in and start the car. Drusilla looked out the window, her mind whirling with questions, but something stopped her from asking any of them outright.

She took a deep breath and turned to look at him. The darkness of the SUV's cab didn't help her at all. It brought her mind back to the forest, the shapes of the trees, and the outline of the Horseman on his white steed in the moonlight.

An icy shiver ran down her back.

"Are you quite alright?"

Drusilla tried to tell Ichabod she was fine but she was too emotionally and physically exhausted to even try to lie. "No, not really."

"I can still take you home," Ichabod replied, carefully. "No shame in calling in sick today."

"No," Drusilla said, crossing her arms.

Being all alone in an enormous house would do her more harm than good. At least at work, Drusilla could distract herself.

You know it's bad when I'd rather carve up bodies than stay home, she thought ruefully to herself.

"I want to know what the hell is going on," she finally asked.

Drusilla could see just enough to catch Ichabod tightening his grip on the steering wheel.

"You should have mentioned that you weren't common," Ichabod said, chuckling bitterly. "It would have made things a lot easier."

"Boy, you better not be calling me basic!"

Ichabod shook his head in disbelief. "Common?" he asked, " As in non-supernatural?"

Blinked, Drusilla's mouth fell open in shock, "Supernatural?!"

"You come from a family of witches, and you're one too." Ichabod rolled his eyes. "Didn't you take the Magnus test?

"What the hell is the Magnus Test?"

Ichabod took a deep breath. "On their thirteenth birthday, witches must take a mandatory test of power. The amount of power you possess is tested to see if you're a witch or common."

"I never took any test like that."

Ichabod paused and gave her a long, penetrating stare. Something inside of her squirmed as she thought about the rush of fire in her veins and the orange energy that had appeared in her hands. Dr. Drusilla Van Tassel was a doctor, a woman of science.

"If my family members were witches, I would have definitely noticed." Drusilla said, " Witches don't exist."

"A witch is a person who has magical powers," Ichabod replied. "The last time I checked, you repelling an undead Hessian soldier 30 meters counts as a 'magical power.'"

"I am *not* a witch!" she shouted.

Drusilla's eyes went wide as a burst of orange energy burst from her hands at the same time. Ichabod yelped, and the car swerved in and out of the lane. The pickup truck behind them honked its horn.

"Look where you're going!" Drusilla screeched, reaching out to stop herself from slamming headfirst into the dashboard.

"Can you turn off the sodding fireworks?"

"I don't know how!"

"Your father didn't teach you how to control your powers?" Ichabod demanded.

Her father was a devoted man who practically lived in the church. "He wasn't a witch, and this was the first time this." Drusilla pointedly looked down at her glowing hands. "has ever happened to me!"

Ichabod turned and gave a long, piercing look. He breathed in deeply and let out a sigh. "Just take it easy. Your magic is obviously tied to your emotions."

"*Take it easy?!*" Drusilla asked incredulously. "How can I be calm in this situation?"

"Please," Ichabod replied through clenched teeth, "Take a deep breath."

Drusilla wanted to tell Ichabod to go fuck himself, but she didn't have a better idea. So, she closed her eyes and took a deep breath. She struggled with the power inside of her; the heat of it felt blistering enough to scorch her insides. She took another deep breath and then another, counting to ten, then twenty. By the time Drusilla got to fifty, her breathing had slowed and the fire inside of her had gradually faded into dull embers.

"Why is this happening to me?" Drusilla felt like her nicely ordered life was spiraling out of control. "Why is it everything's gone to shit since you came back to town? And why the hell are you even here, anyway?"

"I'm a Paladin," Ichabod said through gritted teeth.

"What? Like from Dungeons and Dragons?" Drusilla scoffed.

"My mother is a common who lives in this town and it's my duty to protect the commons from supernaturals," Ichabod said, ignoring her pointedly. Until the undead Horseman is stopped, everyone in Sleepy Hollow is in danger."

"Do you even hear yourself?" Drusilla asked. "You are not some superhero, and your gun sure as hell didn't stop it."

"More effective than your magic," Ichabod shot back. "Lucky for you, my sources informed me about a Horseman sighting."

Drusilla's nostrils flared. "Well, I didn't know magic existed until 45 minutes ago, so cut me some slack."

Ichabod spun into the parking lot and abruptly parked. Then he angrily unlatched his seat belt and turned to her. "What the hell is your problem?"

"Uh, I just saw my sister's best friend get beheaded and was chased through the preserve by an ax-wielding madman?"

"No, not that." Ichabod waved it away. "You've had a stick up your arse since I came back."

"Oh, you're one to fucking talk, Ichabod," Drusilla snarled back, "You've hardly been prince charming yourself."

Ichabod ran a hand over his face. "I need your help, and you need mine."

Drusilla snorted. "I don't need your help."

"You don't know anything about magic," Ichabod said, flailing his hands. You're an untrained witch, and it was your father's duty as Sleepy Hollow's Tiraunt to train you. It appears that Katrina, his heir, has failed both you and the town."

"Tiraunt?"

Ichabod pinched the bridge of his nose, "Coven leader."

Drusilla was at a loss for words. Ichabod has completely lost his mind or maybe she was still asleep, and this was some nightmare. Drusilla was tempted to pinch herself.

None of this made sense. The common ground between her father and sister was their dedication to the church. During their childhood, both sisters spent a considerable amount of time sitting in the pews of the Old Dutch Church.

"Why–" Drusilla's voice shook. She wished to deny it, but Drusilla remembered the power she had held between her fingertips just a few minutes ago. "Why would they keep this from me?"

She despised the pitying look Ichabod gave her. Drusilla had experienced enough pity from others for a lifetime. "You are common. The supernatural world's secrecy code is the Conclave's primary law."

Drusilla frowned, "The Conclave?"

"The council that governs the supernatural world," Ichabod explained. "They make the laws and the Paladins enforce them."

Drusilla groaned, she had suddenly learned about this entirely new world she had been dropped into.

"Since you were an outsider, your family had no choice but to comply. Your father and sister could have lost their lives and their territory if they had told you. " Ichabod tapped his fingers on the steering wheel. "My best guess is that they erased your memories."

"No–" Drusilla feeling sick, to her stomach. "They wouldn't do that."

"They wouldn't have any choice." Ichabod reminded her kindly.

Despite Ichabod's explanation, she didn't feel any better. She didn't want to believe that her family would do that to her. A part of her prayed that Ichabod lying. *What if he is telling the truth?* Drusilla once again felt like an outsider in her family.

Her father was her lifeline once Ichabod left. Drusilla expected for Katrina to push her aside. It's been something she's been doing since they hit middle school. Drusilla was labeled as the weird nerd, while Katrina was considered the cool kid. Her father was the one who told her she was perfect just the way she was. He supported her interests in anime, books, cars, and horses.

She was gifted a Lincoln Continental by her father on her sixteenth birthday. She has spent many happy Saturdays working under the hood of her car with him. The Lincoln was now in bits and pieces.

Her eyes stung with unshed tears.

Now, she discovered a world that her family had intentionally kept hidden from her. Drusilla felt too raw to have an immediate confrontation with Katrina.

After a deep breath, She turned slowly to Ichabod. "Why do you want to help me? Aren't hunters supposed to want to kill people like me?"

"Whatever you do?" Ichabod said with a wince. "Never call another Paladin a hunter."

"Why?"

Ichabod pinched the bridge of his nose. "Only hunters kill indiscriminately. Paladins only kill supernaturals that are a threat to commons or risk commons discovering the supernatural world. The Horseman is risking both."

"Okay, if you don't want to kill me, what do you want?"

Ichabod might have tried to save her, but he was supposedly a Paladin. And despite Drusilla's earlier protests, she had some type of power that now made her part of his world–his crazy, supernatural world, one with rules that Paladins like Ichabod had to enforce.

"I have been hunting the Horseman since I got here, but as you can see, none of my common weaponry works. They're blessed silver alloy bullets. I've taken down many werewolves, vampires, goblins, and ghouls with these bullets, but the Horseman?" Ichabod shook his head. "It barely kept him down."

"Apparently only powerful magic can stop him," Ichabod shook his head. "And Katrina refuses to speak to me."

Wonder why, Drusilla thought sarcastically to herself. She crossed her arms and glared at him. "You said that Katrina is the Tiraunt, so that means she has to have a coven."

Drusilla tried to think about Katrina and her friends being witches. If Katrina was a witch, her friends would probably be the most likely to be in her coven. But that didn't make sense. Denis and now his wife Saundra had been both killed by the Horseman. If they were magical, wouldn't they still be alive?

"No, Katrina was the only one and now you two are the only ones left."

Drusilla's eyes went wide, "How is that possible?"

"Your coven used to be a good mix between family and witches residing within the territory. Your great-grandfather shut out anyone who wasn't blood family. And well–"

The Van Tassel family had mostly died out, with the exception of a few distant cousins who lived in the Netherlands.

This is down to Katrina and me, Drusilla thought to herself. She wanted to scream and pretend that none of this was happening.

"If we work together, we can stop the Horseman—before it kills someone else."

Drusilla gave a bitter laugh. "Absolutely not. I'm not risking everything I worked for just to help an amateur sleuth. I'll figure it out on my own." She undid her seat belt and started to get out.

As Ichabod grabbed her arm, Drusilla stared angrily at him.

"Why are you being so damn stubborn?" Ichabod growled.

"Because I don't trust you," Drusilla replied. "Thanks for your help in the woods and for telling me all of this. This is too much! After sixteen years of not hearing a word from you. You come back to town and tell me that everything I've known about my life is a lie? So, I'm supposed to stop what I'm doing and help you? And trusting you before didn't exactly go well. So maybe I'm a witch or this is just hallucination from sleep deprivation but the one thing I do know for certain is that *you* are a snake in the grass."

"That's harsh, Drusilla." Ichabod frowned. "Weren't you the one who ghosted *me*?"

Drusilla's fists tightened as she fought the urge to punch him in the throat. This man had used her until he was satisfied, then threw her away like trash.

"Fuck you!" She jerked out of his grasp and hurried out of the car.

"Drusilla!" he called out.

"Why don't you do what you do best, Ichabod?" Drusilla shouted as she walked away. "Run to Katrina."

Nine

In The Dead Of Night

Drusilla struggled to accept the reality of magic and the supernatural, despite the overwhelming evidence that a secret magical existed and now she was suddenly thrust into the middle of it.

Upon arriving at her office, Drusilla immediately called Katrina, but once again, it went straight to voicemail. When her shift ended, Drusilla was going to take an Uber to her sister's house. She was determined to get answers, by any means necessary.

Only five more hours to go. Despite the trauma of the attack, she had a job to do. She took a deep breath and a long look at Saundra's body. Her gloved fingers hovered over the victim's severed neck.

Drusilla was used to death and all the nasty consequences of it. Hell, Drusilla had had front-row seats to her father's slow, lingering death. Stage four prostate cancer had taken pieces from Baltus Van Tassel bit by bit until he was only a husk of the man he'd once been.

But what happened on that road tonight had been sudden and violent. She couldn't unsee the Horseman's ax falling and how easily it sliced through Saundra's neck.

Denis and Saundra went out of their way to make her school life a living hell. Drusilla's efforts to avoid them did little to reduce enmity between them. Now Saundra was dead, and it had only been luck and some strange power that had kept Drusilla from suffering the same fate herself.

"Are you okay, boss?" Kyndall asked for what seemed like the thousandth time that night. It had taken no time at all for news of the attack to spread through the building.

Drusilla took a deep breath and nodded. "I'm fine."

She pulled herself together as best she could. Drusilla was a grown-ass woman, and she could handle this shit. But her mind still wandered.

Why don't you do what you do best, Ichabod? Run to Katrina. Thinking about it now, she couldn't believe she'd said that to him. She'd been angry and upset and confused. That's not to say that she hadn't *meant* what she'd said, just that she probably shouldn't have said it out loud.

Drusilla sighed. Everything went back to Ichabod. It was like he was a magnet for chaos. Nothing about him made any sense. Ichabod Crane had shot a supernatural being–the *same* Ichabod who used to sneer at guns, who always hid out at Grimwood even when his father wanted to do some "father-son bonding" via shooting. For Crane, Sr., bonding involved spending hours at the nearby gun range. Surprisingly, it was Ichabod who appeared in the clearing, armed with a Colt M1911 pistol.

Drusilla was startled out of her thoughts as Kyndall hurried through the door, her eyes wide with panic. Drusilla shot to her feet and hurried over to her friend.

"What's wrong?"

Kyndall rushed to Drusilla and put her hands on her shoulder. "Thornton called—"

"Tell him that the results of the examination—"

Kyndall shook her. "No, it's Katrina."

Drusilla snapped her mouth shut. "What? What about my sister?"

"She's missing."

Drusilla could barely keep still as Kyndall drove to Katrina's house. Her best friend was insistent on taking her. God knew how Kyndall had managed to justify her sudden absence to Dr. Willard. She turned to Kyndall, whose face was set in a grim line, her hands gripping the steering wheel in a white-knuckled grip.

Instead of Kyndall's favorite TLC album blasting over her friend's expensive sound system, the trip was quiet and tense. Kyndall turned to Drusilla, her face pinched in obvious concern.

"You okay, boss?" she asked.

Drusilla shrugged. "Thanks for taking me."

Kyndall rolled her eyes. "What kind of best friend would I be if I let you catch an Uber?"

Drusilla tried to smile but she was pretty sure it came out more like a grimace. She fidgeted with her fingers.

Please hurry up, Drusilla inwardly urged Kyndall.

Every stoplight along the way tore at her already frayed nerves. *This can't be happening.* She tried to keep herself calm, but inside, Drusilla just wanted to scream. Drusilla shouldn't have gone to work. Her sister wouldn't be missing now if she had listened to her instincts and gone straight to Katrina's house.

Finally, after what seemed like forever, they were pulled up to Hemlock Drive. The once peaceful street was in complete chaos. Neighbors were gawking, phones out to catch every moment. There were a few squad cars outside with their lights flashing, and, god, was that Estelle Cruz in the corner?

'Why was she even here?'

Drusilla winced as she spotted Deputy Hansen trampling Katrina's prized begonias. *Katrina is going to be pissed,* she thought hysterically to herself.

Drusilla couldn't help but feel like she was experiencing deja vu as she hurried out of the car before Kyndall's truck came to a full stop. She pushed past the rubberneckers and hurried up the path.

"Whoa, Doc!" Sheriff Thornton said as he stopped her. "Where do you think you are going?"

Drusilla struggled against him. "My sister—"

"Calm down, Doc."

Drusilla spun on him. "My *sister* is missing, and you want me to calm down!"

"Yes," Sheriff Thornton replied, lifting an eyebrow. "You carrying on like that isn't going to help her."

"Dru!" Kyndall ran over to them.

She threw a look at Dru and then turned to glare at Thornton. Thornton just rolled his eyes, and Drusilla took a deep breath and calmed her tumultuous emotions.

"What happened to Katrina."

Sheriff Thornton released her and pinched the bridge of his nose. "We got a phone call about a noise disturbance. Someone said they heard screaming. The responding officer found the back door off its hinges. The house had been ransacked."

Drusilla's heart sank. *Please god, no,* she prayed to a god she didn't even believe in. *Not my sister.* But out loud, she calmly asked, "So you didn't find her body?"

"No." Sheriff Thornton shook his head. "We're still looking for Katrina."

Out of the corner of her eye, she saw a flash of red. Drusilla turned just in time to see a CSI technician walk out of her sister's house with a transparent evidence bag in hand. Inside there was something covered in a huge crimson stain that Drusilla immediately suspected was blood.

Sheriff Thornton and Kyndall followed her gaze, and Kyndall gasped. "You don't think—"

Drusilla felt sick to her stomach, her eyes stinging with unshed tears. She spun back around and glared up at Thornton. "I thought—"

Sheriff Thornton threw out his hands, "There was a sign of struggle, but..." He sighed and put his hands on Drusilla's shoulder. "Didn't you say that we shouldn't make assumptions? Something about that is how mistakes are made?"

The Sheriff's parroting of her words caused Drusilla to feel a surge of impotent rage.

"This isn't an assumption," Drusilla jerked away. Don't you find it suspicious that someone tried to kill me tonight? And now my sister is missing!"

She had already lost her parents; now Katrina was the only person she had left. And she had just come so close to death. As much as Drusilla wanted to chalk up the entire episode in the woods to fucked up brain chemistry and trauma, Drusilla was sure that after failing to catch her, the Horseman shifted his focus to her sister.

Kyndall put her arm around her and squeezed.

"Wh-what can I do to help?" Drusilla asked weakly. "I can join the search party."

"Yeah," Kyndall piped up. "Just tell us when and where."

Drusilla threw her a grateful smile.

"No can do. You need to stay as far away from this case as possible," Thornton sternly replied.

"What?" Drusilla said, crossing her arms. "Since when can't family join a search party?"

"Since now." Thornton shook his head. "You were already too close to Carters We all know how tight those two and Katrina were. Since you are her sister, there is now a clear conflict of interest."

"It's not like she's asking to be a part of this investigation," Kyndall pointed out.

"There are too many eyes on this whole thing." Sheriff Thornton sighed. "And now with Katrina missing...You're off this case altogether. Willard is taking this over himself."

"*What?*" Drusilla and Kyndall both shouted.

"Just go home, Doc," Thornton said, patting her on the shoulder. "I'll let you know when I find anything."

Drusilla felt sick to her stomach as she watched Thornton turn and walk back inside her sister's house. This was her case, and he had removed her from it. Drusilla knew firsthand these people didn't understand what they were missing. They had no chance of stopping the Horseman or of finding her sister.

"*My Brom was lying in that godforsaken preserve for hours while the sheriff was probably sitting his ass at the donut shop.*" At that moment, she realized Katrina had been right. Sheriff Thornton only saw her as some hysterical woman who needed to be put up on a shelf. She was not about to let what happened to Brom happen to her sister.

Lucky for her, Drusilla knew exactly who could help her.

Ten

The Pieces of Us

Drusilla made the drive up I-87, squirming in her seat. The steering wheel was still too far away, and the interior of her brand new rental car made her itch. God, she missed her Lincoln, but it would be weeks before the sheriff's department released her car back into her custody. And it would take months to get the Lincoln back in working order.

She took the turnoff and drove down Kemper Avenue headed for Diedrich University. It was a beautiful campus but small. With a sigh of relief, she parked near the Science Center and walked down Prospect Lane to the Thyssen Building. From Drusilla's hasty Google search on her brand new phone, she knew it was the university's administrator center.

It was a beautiful brown brick building that wouldn't have looked all that out of place among the rest of the stately homes of Sleepy Hollow. She walked past a few students and made her way inside. Drusilla stopped in front of the receptionist's desk. Behind it was an elderly white woman typing on a computer.

"Excuse me."

The receptionist looked up from her computer, "Yes, can I help you?"

"I'm looking for Professor Crane. He's teaching Foundations of Western Culture?"

Even though Drusilla was hitting her mid-thirties, she must still look young enough to pass as a college student because the receptionist didn't ask questions, just gave her directions to his classroom in the humanities building. Unfortunately for her, it was still a bit of a walk, and she hoped she'd make it there in time to catch him. With a sigh, Drusilla buttoned up her large tan overcoat and started her trek.

Diedrich University in real life was just as beautiful and picturesque as those glossy photos on their website. It was a mix of old-world elegance with new modern buildings. The atmosphere was decidedly chill and more low-key than Cornell had been. As she strode across the campus, Drusilla idly listened to a group of students chattering excitedly with each other about Andy Warhol and his contribution to the art world. For some reason, it helped ease her nerves a little–but only a little.

Drusilla finally made it to the humanities building and easily found Ichabod's lecture hall. When she carefully opened the door, she saw that the room was half-full, with students dotted sparsely around the lecture hall. Ichabod stood in front of a huge projector, not even close to the lectern, as he spoke passionately to his students about Hamlet.

She quickly took a seat in the back row, where there were only two other people sitting. Her mouth quirked in a smile as she settled down to watch Ichabod.

"Of all of Shakespeare's plays," he said, "Hamlet is still the most controversial after all this time. Its themes of revenge and familial betrayal are captivating because they're universal. Most of us have dealt with the impotent rage that comes with deception."

As Ichabod eagerly explained, his long arms flailed animatedly, waving at a still image of David Tennant playing Hamlet.

Drusilla turned to watch the students. To her surprise, many of them weren't taking notes or even playing on their phones. Ichabod had their complete attention.

"Hamlet allows us to see the folly of revenge," he continued. "Shakespeare doesn't hide from the ugliest parts of humanity, and we should take it as a lesson. Instead of hiding from our darkness, we should confront it and overcome it."

Drusilla saw a woman two rows down lick her lips, her eyes completely rapt on Ichabod's every movement. Her camera was out as she took a photo. Drusilla glowered down at her, her mouth pinching into a firm line.

I'm not jealous. Drusilla forced herself to unclench her fists. *I am not.*

Ichabod smiled, but it wasn't at any one person; this was the smile of a man in his element. "Media such as this is an emotional catharsis; it speaks to the most primal of our impulses as humans. From The Oresteia to The Count of Monte Cristo, revenge stories are an enduring story archetype."

Every time Drusilla encountered Ichabod, she found a recent change in him. She missed the days when they were still sneaking bottles of Jack Daniels under the bleachers and debating which was the best horror film ever made. Inwardly, she chuckled at how angry Ichabod got over her love for Evil Dead. He would puff up like a startled chicken every time she quoted her favorite lines from that movie. While Drusilla had quietly put up with Ichabod's love for Hitchcock movies, Ichabod could never understand why she would pick such a campy movie over his beloved Shadow of a Doubt.

Yet this man in front of her was no longer the boy with hands and feet too big for his thin narrow body. Ichabod had turned into something both beautiful and strange–a man who would look perfect on Katrina's arm.

Drusilla frowned and looked down at her hands. Katrina was missing. Her sister could be dead, her death just another murder to fuel Sleepy Hollow's gossip mill, an urban legend to be discussed in whispers and speculation. And here she was, letting her lingering jealousy and this damnable attraction impede her purpose.

Drusilla had to find her sister and stop the Horseman before he killed again, and nothing else mattered.

Drusilla was startled out of her thoughts as the students started packing up. The woman from earlier hurried down the stairs to talk to Ichabod. She giggled and tucked a strand of hair behind her ear.

Drusilla gritted her teeth and looked away.

Finally, the woman left, leaving Ichabod and Drusilla alone in the cavernous lecture hall– she waited for him to say something. He silently continued to pack up his laptop and his books. Ichabod had to have seen her, but he still said nothing.

With a put-upon sigh, Drusilla got up and made her way down the stairs. Ichabod paid her no attention, and she bit her lip.

"Crane."

Ichabod finally stopped and turned to her. "It's Doctor Crane."

Drusilla just barely stopped herself from rolling her eyes. "Dr. Crane," she corrected herself. "Can I have a moment of your time?"

Ichabod gave her a long, piercing stare. "Very well." Without another word, he walked around the desk and up the stairs. Drusilla stood there for a moment, staring at his retreating back. Ichabod abruptly stopped and called over his shoulder, "Are you coming?"

Drusilla huffed as she hurried to follow him, her short legs barely able to keep up with his long strides. She followed him through a labyrinth of hallways until Ichabod stopped in front of a plain door. He opened it, stepped back, and ushered in.

The office was *tiny*. Her closet at Grimwood was bigger than this. A large chestnut wood desk took up the majority of the space. On Ichabod's wall, his undergraduate degree from NYU and PH.D. from Oxford were hung side by side. There were tall piles of books on every available surface, more than she expected for such a small space.

Behind the desk was a small window that looked out into the Quad.

Drusilla was pretty sure that most adjunct professors just got a nice cubicle but leave it to Ichabod Crane to find a way to get his own office.

"Please take a seat." He gestured to a steel folding chair and then made his way to his desk and set his things down.

"What can I do for you, Doctor?" Ichabod asked, sitting down and steepling those long, elegant fingers together.

"I know that I have been nothing but a bitch to you," Drusilla started. She hated to admit it, but Ichabod had been right all along. Had she listened to him instead of being controlled by her high school trauma, Katrina might still be safe. "I'm sorry for all the shit I said, but I need your help."

Ichabod raised an eyebrow and waited silently for her to continue.

"Katrina is missing," Drusilla replied curtly. "And I think the Horseman has her."

Ichabod's eyes went wide, "What?"

Drusilla took a long breath. Her emotions were all over the place, and she couldn't believe it had been only a couple of hours since she got the news. But she needed to be calm and rational or else she'd never find her sister. So as clinically as she could–as if Drusilla was just giving a report to Sheriff Thornton and not the man that took her virginity on the floor of an ancient-looking cabin–she told him everything she knew.

"I feared something like this would happen," he said when she'd finished.

"What do you mean?" Drusilla demanded.

Ichabod went over to a book cart and pulled out an old leather journal with dull yellow pages. "I found a journal in Rochester that belonged to Pieter Van Tassel."

"Okay?" Drusilla asked, frowning as she picked up the journal. She flipped through the pages, and it was, of course, all written in Dutch. "Why are you looking into my family history?"

"Katrina was meant to be the last Van Tassel witch." Ichabod ruefully replied. "Nonetheless, you are a witch of considerable power. I wanted to know what other things your family got wrong."

The slight to her family made Drusilla angry, but she recognized that he had a point. Both her sister and father had dropped the ball on this. And Ichabod was left to pick up the pieces.

"Katrina has not been as supportive as I had anticipated." Ichabod pinched the bridge of his nose, "The horseman succeeded in taking down a Tiraunt. "

"Bad?"

"Quite," He agreed then took a deep breath, slid his laptop out of his bag, and booted it up. After clicking on the mouse pad for a few minutes, he spun the laptop around.

Drusilla froze, dropping the journal to the floor as she stared at the image of the painting on the screen. It was a painting of a Black couple. From the clothing, it was obvious that this was painted in the 18th century. But it was the man that immediately caught her attention. He was dressed in a long coral-colored jacket, breeches, and tricorn hat. He was tall, with short kinky hair, brown eyes, and a neatly trimmed beard.

"This is Pieter Van Tassel," Ichabod said.

"I know," Drusilla whispered, her eyes fixed on the achingly familiar face.

"How?" Ichabod asked, frowning.

Drusilla finally turned away from the laptop to meet Ichabod's eyes. "Because I dreamed about him."

Eleven

The Branches of Fate

Drusilla should be used to this feeling. As if she was Alice, falling through the rabbit hole.

She couldn't quite look away from the painting. Her eyes traveled to the person next to Pieter, and there was something familiar about them as well.

They were beautiful, dressed in an elaborate yellow dress that went well against their sepia-toned skin. Their long, curly, dark brown hair was pulled into an elaborate updo. Yet, it was something about their round-shaped eyes and the shape of their turn-up nose that drew Drusilla's attention the most.

"Dru—Doctor?" Ichabod asked. "Are you quite alright?"

Drusilla nodded. "Wh-who is that?" She pointed to the woman.

Ichabod lifted an eyebrow, but he turned back to the laptop. "That's Mathilde Van Tassel. His spouse. There's not a lot known about them." He shrugged. "Mathilde was a slave, and Pieter fell in love with them. He managed to convince their owner to sell her to him."

Drusilla wrinkled her nose. "So, she was the property of one of my ancestors?"

Ichabod shook his head. "No, he freed her. It wasn't unheard of back then. Unfortunately, with Pieter being a Van Tassel, it was quite the scandal."

Drusilla bit her lip. "I don't understand why. I mean, it's obvious that he was biracial. He was probably a son of a slave, too."

"Correct." Ichabod sighed. "Pieter was a freedman who immigrated from the Netherlands to America. He was the first Black man to own a shipping company."

As Ichabod switched tabs on his computer to some newspaper clippings in Dutch, she asked, "By the way, since when do you know Dutch?"

Ichabod shrugged and looked away. "Since my freshman year of uni." Then he coughed and quickly changed the subject. "We'll never know what made him sell his shipping business, but when he came over to America, he was very wealthy."

Drusilla didn't know how to feel. Her father was such a history buff. One of his favorite pastimes was antiquing and going to estate sales. But he never talked about their own family's history. Drusilla had chalked it up to her father being ashamed that their ancestors were slave owners.

Drusilla frowned. "Wait a second, what about Hendrick Van Tassel? You know? The man that has his name on half of the stuff in town?"

"Hendrick was a distant cousin of Pieter's, and there was no love lost between the two."

"So why was there such an enormous scandal over Pieter marrying Mathilde?"

"Even back then, anything involving a Van Tassel was big news in this town. And a Van Tassel marrying a slave? It was unheard of." Ichabod shook his head. "Mathilde was a bit of a rebel. First, they were literate, which was illegal back then. But then, in Pieter's diaries, he mentions that Mathilde decided they were neither a man nor a woman."

"So, Mathilde was non-binary," Drusilla said, not surprised in the slightest as mentally re-examined her memory of her nightmares.

Drusilla sat back and thought about all of Ichabod's revelations. It was nice to know about her ancestors. Yet, as she put all the clues together, the picture that it painted made her sick to her stomach. What if her dreams were not nightmares, but a glimpse into the past? Her ancestors were the ones who had killed the Horseman and apparently, he was back for revenge.

If that's the case, why did the Horseman kill Denis and Saundra? Although Drusilla couldn't make sense of it, she had a feeling that her dream and the resurrection of the horseman were connected.

Drusilla walked over to the guest chair and shakily sat down.

"Doctor?" Ichabod asked in concern.

Logic told her that Katrina was already dead, but there was something inside of her that screamed that her sister was still alive. Was it some twin instinct–or just denial that she'd lost the last of her family?

Eyes brimming with tears, she thought about their last meeting. Drusilla should have never walked away. She should have been a better sister.

Ichabod hurried over to her and squatted down until they were at eye level. "Doctor?"

She bit her lip. "I haven't been entirely honest with you."

Ichabod just looked at her, his face soft with concern.

Drusilla took a deep breath, "I've been having these nightmares since I was a kid."

"Nightmares?"

"It always starts with being on a horse," Drusilla explained, quietly. "We're…we're running away from the Horseman. But I'm not…I'm not me. I'm them. I'm…Mathilde."

Ichabod had been quietly listening, but now he said, "I don't know what it means, but it must be significant somehow."

"They're just dreams."

"You know, you've been the only person since Mathilde that has been able to stop the Horseman," Ichabod replied, pensively.

"The spell didn't work. The only thing I did was push the Horseman back."

"You're a new witch, and you don't have the benefit of a coven or a mentor," Ichabod pointed out.

"Then how can we stop him?" Drusilla put her face in her hands. "My sister–"

No matter how much research I did on the Horseman, I couldn't figure out how they stopped him initially. By the time he was stopped, the Horseman had already killed hundreds of colonial soldiers.

Ichabod got up and started pacing. Your nightmares suggest that Franklin promised to free the slaves if Mathilde's coven succeeded in stopping the Horseman. He didn't keep that promise, but that's not the point."

He stopped pacing and propped his hip up against the side of his desk. "I don't have all the answers yet, but I can do some more research. Maybe the historical society and some of Franklin's journals will have a clue on how to stop him."

"You think he'd write about the deal that he had with Mathilde's coven?" She asked incredulously. "He had to know people would read his journals."

"Franklin was famous for writing in code," Ichabod said. "There could be something in them that common historians have overlooked."

"Probably didn't want it known that he'd promised to free slaves. Especially since he was homies with George Washington," Drusilla shrugged.

Ichabod stroked his beard, and Drusilla followed the movement of those long, dexterous fingers, her eyes darting every so often to his tempting mouth. Drusilla gasped as Ichabod licked his lips, and she looked up to meet the bastard's eyes, which were twinkling with amusement.

"I think we need to do some research," Ichabod said. "I'll start searching through the online archives, but I think a trip to the library is a good place to start. "

Drusilla sighed. "Okay, well, I'm free for the foreseeable future. Since Dr. Willard took me off this case, I decided it was a good time to use all the PTO I have saved up."

"How about tomorrow at four?" Ichabod asked, "I've only got a few classes then."

"Fine." Drusilla stood up, not daring to look at him.

"Drusilla."

His deep melodic voice, and the crisp tone of his British accent, made her shiver. She closed her eyes and tried to take a deep breath. God, the way he made her body hum should be illegal. And suddenly she could feel his presence behind her, the hotline of his body pressed against her once again, and it made her body tingle in anticipation. Instead of doing what she desired, he decided to simply place a hand on her shoulder

"Please," His voice was rough with some emotion Drusilla didn't want to look too closely into it. "Be careful."

Twelve

The Guilt of the Living

Drusilla woke with her heart pounding in her chest. The ax that had hovered over Mathilde was way too similar to the one from her close encounter with the Horseman.

It was so strange that for years Drusilla had dreamed of being chased across colonial Sleepy Hollow without ever questioning why. Yet, over time, those dreams had progressed into something more.

Drusilla put her head in her hands and tried to breathe. *When did my life get out of control?*

She needed to stay strong. Nothing else mattered to her except finding Katrina.

Drusilla got up and headed into the bathroom. She looked into the mirror, frowning at the dark circles under her eyes. It felt like she hadn't had a good night's sleep in ages.

Drusilla quickly went through her morning absolutions and headed downstairs to start her day. After three cups of coffee and a bowl of cereal. Katrina wasn't here to provide her answers so it was time for Drusilla to approach the most likely source. She walked out of the kitchen and down the hall to the door of her father's study.

Her fingers were poised above the brass doorknob. Drusilla had always known that this room was off-limits, and after her father's death, she didn't believe she could handle the enormity of her grief.

It's the reason Drusilla has avoided moving to the master bedroom. Drusilla has to accept that her father will never come home, and she is alone.

This was something she finally had to face.

Drusilla opened the door. She could nearly smell the cedarwood of her father's cologne as she stood in the doorway.

The walls were lined with tall bookshelves made of golden brown oak. The shelves overflowed with leather-bound books. At the center of the room was a rectangular executive desk, dark walnut brown in color. A red Persian rug lay beneath the desk. Beyond the desk was a large bay window that gave a view of the estate's manicured lawn. From afar, Drusilla spotted Hobbs leading the horses towards the nearby pens.

Shaking her head, Drusilla quickly crossed the room. Her fingers glided across the smooth wood until they reached the empty leather high-back chair. Drusilla imagined her father sitting there. His huge body would be crouched over his paperwork. She could almost see his short and neat gray hair, serious dark eyes, and thick black rectangular frames.

Drusilla's eyes stung with tears. *I miss him so much!* Drusilla took a deep breath and tried to get her emotions under control. If she began crying now, she would never stop.

Drusilla began rifling through his desk. The neatness of her father's desk didn't come as a surprise to her. Baltus Van Tassel was always known for his fastidiousness.

Nothing was interesting. She came across numerous invoices for horse feed, veterinarian bills, and other common ranch expenses. Along with that, there were office supplies and a stack of paid bills.

Drusilla dedicated the next few hours to combing through the rest of the study. She went through his laptop, his file cabinets, his old Rolodex, and every drawer or cabinet in the room.

There was nothing to suggest that her father was a secret witch. Drusilla was fully prepared to find something embarrassing, such as her father's old copies of Penthouse

The study was immaculate.

Well, this was a colossal waste of my time. Drusilla sighed as she walked over and dropped into an oversized red chintz chair that sat next to the large black fireplace.

On top of a pile of books he forgot to return to the shelf, was an old copy of The Hollow Herald. Drusilla smiled softly as she reverently touched the spines of the books. There were well-loved copies of If Beale Street Could Talk by James Baldwin, Their Eyes Were Watching by Zora Neale Hurston, and The Souls of Black Folk by W.E.B. DuBois.

Drusilla inherited her love of reading from her father. Although her father had a liking for Black classic literature, Drusilla preferred horror novels from writers like Victor Lavalle, Tananarive Due, and Octavia Butler.

Drusilla got up and put the books back where they belonged. While sliding Zora Neale Hurston's book onto the shelf, her hands grew warm and began to glow. Suddenly, the section of the bookcase was gone.

Two manila folders were sitting in their place. Drusilla hastily grabbed the folders, and then abruptly the books reappeared as if nothing had occurred.

One of them had her sister's name and the other had Drusilla's. Drusilla glanced at the papers and noticed the date. The reports were written on September 13, 2002, just one day after Drusilla and Katrina's thirteenth birthday.

```
Subject: Katrina Jenever Van Tassel
Magnus Score 7.8
```

The paper discussed a series of tests that evaluated Katrina's power and control. Drusilla switched over to the other folder.

```
Subject: Drusilla Nicole Van Tassel
Magnus Score:  2.3
```

Her gaze went straight to the last line.

Miss Van Tassel's abilities are deficient and are only within common ranges. She shows no sign of outstanding ability or power. We recommend immediate erasure.

"Erasure," Drusilla muttered to herself. She tried to remember the period around that birthday. Drusilla recollected the enormous birthday party Baltus had thrown for her and Katrina. Drusilla has very few happy memories with her sister before she transformed into the Queen Bee caricature she is today.

But the day after? Her father drove Drusilla and Katrina somewhere, but Drusilla's recollection was foggy after that.

Drusilla felt sick, "Fuck, Ichabod was right."

Upon arriving at Tarrytown, Drusilla was a bundle of nerves as she drove towards the Warner Library. Her father lied to her and erased her memories because she was common. It ruined all the good memories Drusilla had of him. Although she could understand Katrina's silence, but why couldn't she forgive her father's actions? She started to question what parts of her life were real and which ones were made up.

While trying to park, Drusilla let out a sigh of annoyance. Apparently, everyone and their mama need to visit the library that day. When she finally pulled into a free spot, she hurried towards the entrance but couldn't quite make herself go in yet.

The library was a large, white, rectangular building, and its classical architecture made the whole place look timeless. She took a moment to ground herself, then, with a sigh, collected her satchel and opened the heavy brass-plated door.

She walked past the receptionist's desk, her heavy boots thumping against the shiny white linoleum floors, and into the reading room then over to the work-study section of the library. Her eyes traveled around the room, seeing quite a few college students huddled together over books and some older people sitting at the computers. Then she spotted Ichabod sitting at an empty table near the back, a stack of books next to him.

These days, Ichabod was always stylish, but today he wore a crisp, tailored white shirt that showed off his entirely too distracting broad shoulders. The sleeves were rolled up to his elbows, giving her a nice view of his tan, muscular forearms. Then add the tweed waistcoat on top of that, and that man looked entirely too fine for a simple trip to the library.

Focus, Dru, she chided herself as she walked over to him and dropped her bag on the table. Ichabod hit his knee on the table and swore in surprise.

"Ssh!" the librarian said, and Drusilla winced. She silently mouthed sorry to the librarian before quickly taking a seat.

"Was that necessary?" Ichabod hissed. Drusilla considered making Ichabod the scapegoat for her terrible mood but ultimately decided not to. She threw him an apologetic look, "I'm sorry."

Looking up, his hazel eyes were huge behind his wire-framed glasses

"What's wrong?" Ichabod asked, immediately. "What happened?"

After sighing heavily in defeat, Drusilla retrieved two manila folders from her bag and handed them to him. "Read it," Drusilla paused, "Please."

Raising an eyebrow, Ichabod flipped through the pages and then paused. "This is Lonhẽian. This language is magical, but only a few covens have used it. I've never seen a Magnus test written in this language before."

"I think it's the same one from my dream, " Drusilla bit her lip.

Ichabod shook his head. Only magicians can read and speak magical languages. I'm scared that I'm too common to understand them.

Suppressing a sigh of frustration, Drusilla pulled the folders towards her. "You were right! Both my sister and I were tested."

"So, what were the results?"

Drusilla crossed her arms, "Katrina got a 7.8 on the test."

Ichabod gave a low whistle, "As I suspected, Katrina is pretty powerful."

Drusilla huffed, "I was only a 2.3".

Ichabod froze, his mouth dropping open. "Surely, you are taking the piss!"

Drusilla went to her file and tapped the number. Ichabod shook his head, "What I saw back there was not a 2.3"

Drusilla only shrugged, "Maybe I'm a late bloomer?"

Ichabod just stared at her for a long moment before he finally said, "Late bloomers are rare, but it does happen."

Drusilla groaned and put her head in her hands. "I know my family had to keep it from me on pain of death. But it's not making me feel any better, you know?? I just don't know what to believe anymore."

"Well, the first step is to stop the Horseman," Ichabod said, as he took out a tiny orange bottle and shook out two pills.

Drusilla stared at the pill bottle.

"Adderall," Ichabod snorted. "Unfortunately, I didn't get to grow out of my ADHD."

"Okay," Drusilla pointedly looked at the stack of books. She picked up one of the books. "*Folklore and Myths from The American Colonies*," she read out loud. Then she frowned and flipped through the other books. "Have you found anything?"

Ichabod pursed his lips. "No. I was hoping to find similarities in all the different myths about the Horseman. Most of it is utter rubbish, but the consistencies within different myths can give us a clue. Myths about horsemen that hunt in the night are old. Some go back to the Wild Hunt and the old myths from Western Europe. In particular, Gallic and Norse mythology."

Drusilla took out her laptop and her notebook. "The Horseman couldn't be that old, could it?"

Ichabod shook his head. "In the supernatural community, it's pretty well known that the British monarchy was attempting to use the occult to win the war against the colonies. But if the Horseman was indeed the manifestation of some old deity, I doubt it would travel to America. Gods tend to stick to their territory."

Drusilla snorted so loudly that she got some dirty looks thrown at her. "Gods are real?"

Ichabod nodded. "I know a mate that's had some encounters with them." He shuddered. "It didn't turn out well." He coughed and adjusted his glasses. "No, this was something created by the British supernaturals. Most likely a powerful coven or magician."

"Which is why Franklin went to Mathilde's coven," Drusilla said, tapping her fingers on the table. "Learn anything more about the deal between those two?"

He frowned. "No, but I'm still searching."

"So why don't you continue searching Franklin's journals for clues and I look up anything that can tell us more about the Horseman?"

"Sounds like a plan." Ichabod handed her a notebook. "Here are all the notes that I've made so far."

Drusilla nodded her thanks and got to work.

Thirteen

The Worth of Your Doorway

It didn't take long for both Drusilla and Ichabod to get lost in their research. With all the baggage between them, Drusilla had expected to feel uncomfortable. She assumed that their past had snuffed out any ounce of camaraderie between them. However, to her surprise, it was almost like old times.

Drusilla felt a tug of nostalgia for those days. Back then, they had spent most of their lunch hours in libraries, reading or talking quietly under the stern glare of the school librarian. They both had been bullied relentlessly by Brom and his friends, but even with all of that, things had been much simpler when they were younger.

Time passed pleasantly despite the circumstances. Drusilla skimmed through books, taking notes and cross-referencing Ichabod's findings with her own. Ichabod hadn't been wrong about the Horseman myths; there were quite a lot of them. But the few similarities between them weren't helpful at all.

Once she realized there was nothing to be found there, Drusilla decided to search the historical census, trying to find anything about Pieter or Mathilde, or any hint of who the other members of Mathilde's coven were. Sadly, that proved to be even less fruitful.

"Ugh, I got nothing," Drusilla said, knocking her head against the heavy tome.

When she looked over at him, she was surprised to see Ichabod giving her a soft smile, though she might've been imagining it. Her heart thumped heavily in her chest, and she quickly looked away.

Drusilla noticed it was past sunset, and she checked her watch. "Shit, it's nearly nine. The library will close soon."

Ichabod took off his glasses and massaged the bridge of his nose. "I've got nothing. You?"

Drusilla shrugged. "Nothing more than what you initially found. The slave records and census data we need aren't here. We might have more luck at the historical society."

"You might be right," he conceded. "There are so many missing pieces."

"That is how investigations usually work," she said. "It's slow going until you get a lead."

"This is hardly my first case, and I usually enjoy the research but—" Ichabod sighed. "For the first time, I have something to lose. I wish I could convince my mother to take a vacation until this is solved."

Drusilla snorted "Analyn go on vacation now that you're home?" She shook her head. "You're the sun she orbits around, you know that?"

Ichabod looked away, "I care about her deeply."

"Do you?" Drusilla said. "Because you have a shitty way of showing it."

"What is *that* supposed to mean?" Ichabod crossed his arms and glared at her.

Drusilla rubbed her forehead. She was exhausted, and she didn't want to fight with him. Putting her hands up, she said, "I'm sorry, I shouldn't have said that."

"No, you know what?" Ichabod threw up his hands. "How about for once, you speak your mind?"

Drusilla was thankful that Ichabod was helping her but on the other hand, she hated how much Ichabod took his mother for granted. Analyn had taken Drusilla under her wing, checked up on her, and treated her not like her son's discarded friend but like her own daughter. Beyond her hurt feelings, Drusilla wanted Analyn to be happy.

She gave a deep sigh. "You may have had your reasons for leaving," she conceded, thinking about her own choice to stay in Sleepy Hollow after her own father's death. "But maybe you could see your mother more often. Hell, Analyn would be overjoyed if you called or sent more letters. You're the only family she has left."

Drusilla's mind immediately back to Katrina. But as Ichabod sat silently, waiting for her to continue, she tried to shove her doubts and fears to the side.

"You still have a parent that loves you," Drusilla said. "I don't. My dad is gone, Katrina is missing, and my mother..." Drusilla trailed off because the less said about her mother, the better. "You never know how long you have with the people you love. And you can't take that for granted."

For a while, Ichabod didn't say anything. He was quiet for so long that Drusilla thought he was just going to blow her off. Then, finally, he said, "I love my mother. I love her so much, but being back here in Sleepy Hollow is so bloody hard."

Drusilla didn't know what to say to that.

"Do you know what the last thing I said to my father was?" Ichabod asked, startling her. She knew his father was a touchy subject. "I told him I hated him," Ichabod said softly. "And the next thing I knew, he was dead. I—" He looked away. "I was never good enough for him. I was never into sports, had no interest in guns, and I made it pretty clear that I would never follow him into the Army. But even though we were so different, I still loved him, and he went to his grave thinking that I hated him."

"Ichabod—"

"My father grew up here," he said, cutting her off. "And every time I turn the corner, there's some memory of him just waiting for me."

Drusilla nodded. "Yeah, I can understand."

Ichabod stared at her a moment, and then he nodded. "Didn't your father pass earlier this year?"

"Cancer is a bitch." Drusilla gave a bitter laugh. "I love Grimwood, but the place is full of memories of him. You would think that was comforting, but it's not."

There was a cough, and the librarian was walking over to them. "I'm sorry, but the library is closed."

"Sorry, we will get going," Drusilla said, quickly packing her bag. As they walked out of the eerily quiet library and into the cool night air, Drusilla turned to Ichabod. There was so much she wanted to say to him, but in the end, she blurted out, "I think we should talk to Pastor Sparks."

Ichabod cocked his head to the side. "Why?"

Strangely, the Horseman has been targeting Katrina's friends." Drusilla replied, "He wants revenge on my family. So why target her friends? Besides being Katrina's last remaining friend, Pastor Sparks may have information that the others might have shared with him. Either way, there might be a target, and I think it's worth visiting him. "

"It's not just your family that stopped him last time," Ichabod pointed out. These people who died could be descendants of the other members of Mathilde's coven. It's an angle I hadn't thought to pursue until now."

Drusilla shook her head. "I don't know about Katrina's friends being witches. Especially not abolitionist witches."

She thought about all her interactions with Katrina and Brom's friends. They were assholes, but there was nothing magical about them. Yet, Drusilla could be wrong. She had been wrong about her father and Katrina, among other things. Hell, if someone had told her last week that she had the power to repel an ancient, murderous entity, she would've told them to seek help.

Ichabod shrugged. "It's a long shot, but I have some tools that can detect magical signatures."

They quickly made their plans, and with that, Drusilla hurried to her car, her mind whirling from everything Ichabod had told her. Ichabod had been an asshole leaving town like he did, but grief is a strange thing. Drusilla knew that from firsthand experience. They'd been kids back then, and they'd both made stupid mistakes.

As Drusilla drove away, she couldn't quite shake her guilt and unease.

The next day, Drusilla and Ichabod arrived at the Old Dutch Church, one of Sleepy Hollow's oldest historical landmarks. Unlike the rest of the wealthy trappings of the town, the church was a rather simple building, rectangular with a grey tiled roof and a small bell tower on top. The rest of it was light brown fieldstone with one narrow door and a few white arched windows on either side.

In the distance, you could see the top of the gravestones that made up Sleepy Hollow Cemetery.

As Ichabod held the door open for her, she saw the familiar inside of the ancient church, which was just as simple as the outside. There were about a dozen rows of tightly packed white pews facing the altar, which was framed by a wooden gate and a spiral staircase that led up to another pulpit. Behind them in the gallery loomed a large pipe organ.

Next to the spiral staircase, typing away on his laptop at a small desk was Pastor Sparks. His expensive gray suit and laptop both stood out as anachronisms in a church that had gone largely unchanged since it was established in 1697.

"Pastor Sparks?" Drusilla called out.

The man looked up and grinned. When Drusilla and Ichabod went to school with him, he'd simply been Randall Sparks, a defensive lineman for the football team. Back then, with his dirty blond hair, blue eyes, and muscular body, he'd been handsome in that basic white boy way that had most of the girls at school sighing over him. Now, sixteen years later, Pastor Sparks was still trim, but what had been long, wavy hair was now short with a receding hairline, and deep laugh lines and crow's feet made him look a little older than he was.

Damn, this man's my age, and you'd think he was hitting 50, Drusilla thought to herself as Pastor Sparks quickly closed his laptop and hurried over to them.

"Drusilla." His eyes rose as he looked over her shoulder. "By God, is that Icky?"

Ichabod crossed his arms and glowered at the pastor. "It's Ichabod."

Pastor Sparks gave a cough that barely disguised his laughter. "Sorry, *Ichabod*. Didn't realize you were back in town" His blue eyes twinkled as he darted them from Ichabod to Drusilla. "And, of course, the first thing you do is go to Drusilla. You were always as thick as thieves."

"Well, be that as it may—" Ichabod began huffily.

"You here to finally make an honest woman of her?" Pastor Sparks interrupted. "I can give you a discount on my wedding package."

Drusilla groaned and put her hands up. "Stop being an ass, Randy." Her cheeks grew hot in embarrassment. "We're just friends." *And I'm not even sure about that,* she added silently.

Something strange flickered in Ichabod's hazel eyes, something that made her shiver. Then Ichabod looked away and returned his attention to Pastor Sparks. "Pastor, you heard about Katrina?"

Pastor Sparks' grin faded, his eyes dulling with sorrow. "Yeah, I heard about Kat." He shook his head. "It's a goddamn shame."

"We were wondering if you had any clue to her whereabouts?" Ichabod asked.

Pastor Sparks sighed. "I wish I knew."

"Are you sure there's nothing?" Drusilla asked desperately. "You and Kat were friends."

"We've never been that close. I was always closer to Brom." Pastor Sparks shrugged. "And we barely talk anymore after Brom's death. She doesn't really talk to a *lot* of people anymore."

"I knew it was bad," Drusilla said, "but I didn't think—"

The theme song to Jaws blasted through the sanctuary, interrupting them. Pastor Sparks swore under his breath and pulled out his phone. He winced at the display. "I'm sorry that's my wife, I'm going to have to take this."

"We can wait," Drusilla assured him.

The Pastor threw them a forced smile and hurried out of the church, leaving Ichabod and Drusilla alone.

"He's still an insufferable wanker." Ichabod huffed.

Drusilla rolled her eyes. "We're in the Lord's house."

Ichabod snorted. "I'm an atheist, remember?"

"Yeah, I remember your very Catholic mother swearing at you in Tagalog when you told her."

Ichabod rubbed his beard. "Yes, well, Pastor Sparks is *still* an insufferable berk."

Drusilla snorted and walked down the pews, her fingers tracing their chestnut trim. This church was so full of memories. She could see her father and mother still together, her and her sister sitting between them in white dresses, bobby socks, and gleaming patented leather shoes. Together, they had projected the illusion of a perfect family.

She could feel Ichabod's eyes on her, silently following her. It felt like a physical weight between her shoulder blades. Drusilla ignored it and instead focused on her memories. She hummed under her breath to the melody of her favorite lullaby.

"Luonbre fa bierme frue. Saru e reioice bleuque," Drusilla sang to herself as she walked to the small dais.

"Drusilla?" Ichabod called out. Drusilla turned to look at him but she didn't want to stop. The lullaby comforted her and she could she a little more comfort in her life right now.

"Teu iouful depibre. Dache saru teu jue saru delme bierme. Lu mieurd luonbre." While Drusilla sang, a glowing red word suddenly appeared. It was like someone had carved it into the dark wood of the pulpit.

"Wisdom," Drusilla said, reaching out to touch the word. "This means wisdom." Then Drusilla jumped as Ichabod quickly pulled her away. Suddenly, the pulpit broke in two and slid away, revealing a narrow red door.

"What the fuck?" Drusilla asked, shaking her head. "What—"

"Drusilla?" Ichabod asked, concerned.

Drusilla blinked up at Ichabod. "I'm fine. I-I didn't mean for that to happen."

"What type of spell was that?"

Drusilla shook her head, "That wasn't a spell. It was a lullaby."

"That was no ordinary lullaby," Ichabod replied, slowly. "That was a Lonhẽian song."

"I think my dad used to sing this lullaby to me," Drusilla frowned.

Ichabod and Drusilla stared at each other. "Do you think my memories are coming back?"

Ichabod shrugged, "I don't know.

She gestured at the door. "The more important question is, where did this door come from?"

Ichabod followed her gaze and then frowned at her. "What door?"

Drusilla went over and knocked on the door. "You don't see the door right here?"

"Why are you knocking on the pulpit?"

She ignored him, grabbing the knob and pulling the door open.

"Hey, what are you doing?" someone demanded.

Ichabod and Drusilla spun around to see Pastor Sparks standing there.

Drusilla stepped back. "We're just looking around. It's been so long since Ichabod's been in town, and he's interested in this place's history."

Pastor Sparks eyed them suspiciously, then said, "Well, as much as I'd love to give you a history lesson, I need to close up. I still have to meet up with Saundra's and Denis' parents. I'm preparing for their funerals, and there's still so much to be done."

Ichabod opened his mouth, but Drusilla shot him a look, then turned back to the Pastor. "Well, we should be off, then. Thank you for your time."

Drusilla took Ichabod's arm and practically dragged him out of the church to his Range Rover.

Once inside the car, Ichabod asked, "What in the hell was that?"

Drusilla shook her head. "He wasn't going to tell us anything else."

"You don't know that." Ichabod rolled his eyes. "And what about your imaginary door?"

She smirked. "Oh, we're coming back tonight. You didn't think I was going to let our first lead go that easily, did you?"

Ichabod just shook his head and started up the car as Drusilla wondered to herself if she was really going to do this and if she was really going to break into a church. If her father was alive, he'd be horrified. But her father was dead, and Katrina needed her.

And Drusilla would do anything to get her sister back.

Fourteen

When A Drip Becomes A Deluge

Following their conversation with Pastor Sparks, Drusilla and Ichabod went back to the library to continue their research. Ichabod had no classes left for the day, and Drusilla chose to be productive rather than being at home.

Drusilla and Ichabod spent the first hour researching the history of the Old Dutch Church. According to the few books she skimmed through, The Lord of Philipse Manor designed the church in 1685. To make North Tarrytown the county seat, Lord Philispe created a church in the existing village. Ultimately, the

British confiscated The Philispe's property due to their decision to side with the colonies.

There were no signs to suggest that the church had any significance beyond being a colonial landmark.

Drusilla pinched her nose and slammed the book shut. She directed her attention to Ichabod who was entirely engrossed in his book, only stopping now and then to jot down notes.

Drusilla picked up another book: The Revolutionary History of the Hudson Valley by Beulah Conner. Her father loved history more than she did, but she did stop to read a chapter about Major John Andre, who was hanged for espionage along with Benedict Arnold. On the other page, black and white illustration of Andre hanging from a weird looking tulip tree that had a heart shaped knot in the middle.

With a sigh, Drusilla skimmed through the rest of the book, unable to concentrate. Her thoughts returned to the church and its magical door. Drusilla was finding magical secrets everywhere she went lately and Drusilla was exhausted.

She longed for the predictability of her past life.

Yet, there was another part of her, a much bigger part of her, that wanted to know the whole truth once and for all.

She thought again about their encounter with Pastor Sparks. He was acting like his usual douchebag self, which was typical of Katrina and Brom's friends. Yet, it was the way he talked about Katrina that didn't sit right with her. Another thing that kept nagging at her was how the Horseman was singling out Katrina's friends.

Biting her lip, Drusilla took out her laptop. Initially, she searched Google for Katrina, Brom, and their friends. She discovered their Facebook accounts, a handful of Twitter accounts, and Katrina's Instagram account. She also found Brom's old website for his consulting business, and the typical society pages from The Hollow Herald came up.

While scrolling through photos, she noticed several with the five friends, but none stood out. *What was I hoping to find?* Drusilla scoffed to herself. After that, she logged onto the Sherrif's police database.

Drusilla had access to it as a medical examiner, but logging on while on leave could get her in trouble with her boss. Fortunately for her, Drusilla had been in Sheriff Thornton's office multiple times and had seen him enter his code.

The man typed slowly enough for her to remember every key he pressed. Drusilla jotted it down in her notes app. She had a hunch that she would need it at some point.

Drusilla signed in to the police database and entered Katrina's name. There was no record of Katrina contacting the sheriff. She found that strange because Drusilla often had to drag a belligerent Katrina out of the Sherrif's office more than once after Brom died. Nevertheless, there was no mention of it in Brom's case.

Drusilla typed in Brom's name and there was of course his closed case but Drusilla also spotted a link to another case file.

"Ichabod," Drusilla hissed.

His gaze fixed on the book, Ichabod didn't move. Drusilla tapped him on the shoulder. Ichabod looked up and turned to glare at her, "Yes?"

Drusilla rolled her eyes and slid her laptop over to him, "Look at this."

Ichabod sighed and begrudgingly took the laptop. His eyes went wide, "Brom was arrested? It seemed like he fought with Denis and Randy."

"It doesn't make any sense," Drusilla shook her head. "Those three were tights as thieves."

"Maybe they were drunk," Ichabod suggested. "Alcohol makes fools out of most men."

"But why is this the first I am hearing about this?" Drusilla asked. "This would have been the talk of the town."

Re-reading the case file, Ichabod let out a sigh. "Brom is a Van Brunt. It would have been an easy task to hide this with the family's wealth and influence."

"I don't understand how this information will help us find the horseman," Drusilla shrugged, "I thought doing some internet sleuthing would give me some more answers, but I'm just left with more questions. "

Ichabod took her hand and squeezed it, "We are going to find Katrina."

Drusilla knew she should have pushed him away, but she found his reassurance comforting. She felt his long and warm fingers on top of hers. As he ran his thumb along her fingers, Drusilla's heart began to race.

"Thank you," Drusilla said, feeling awkward. The abrupt intimacy did not excuse his past behavior nor did it mean Ichabod would stay after it was all finished. She had to keep up her guard.

Drusilla convinced Ichabod to take a break around one o'clock, and the pair stopped by the Grindhouse Cafe for lunch. It took only 10 minutes to get from The Library to the cafe. The Grindhouse Cafe was a horror theme restaurant that served the best coffee in the county.

The cafe had caused a bit of a fuss when it first opened. Despite it being a hot topic in town meetings and op-eds in The Hollow Herald, Lucretia Riddle, or Lucy as they all knew her, refused to acknowledge it. The cafe was still doing well two years later.

Lucy waved them over as they both entered Grindhouse. Lucy was a fat woman with dark olive skin who had dyed black hair pinned up in Victory rolls, and black cat eyeglasses that matched her black painted lips. She resembled a mix of a plus-sized Morticia Addams and Dita Von Teese.

Lucy's aesthetic was perfectly complemented by the cafe's decor. The cafe was decorated like a 1950s diner that was getting ready for a Halloween party. The tables in the black booths were covered with orange and black spider web tablecloths. They painted the whole register a glossy black with little windows that displayed various desserts.

One wall had a huge orange and black mural of a cemetery where undead arms were reaching out from under the ground.

"Hey, you got a hot date?" Lucy teased.

Drusilla rolled her eyes. "He's just a friend."

"Nice to meet you." Lucy's eyes raked over Ichabod's body, her mouth splitting into a wide grin. "I'm Lucy."

"Uh," Ichabod darted a helpless look at Drusilla, his ears the shade of ripe tomatoes. "Ichabod Crane, nice to meet your acquaintance."

"Can I get a Roosted pumpkin salad, a monster chicken wrap, and a cinnamon latte?" Drusilla asked curtly.

"Sure?" Lucy replied. And as Lucy actually fluttering her eyelashes? Drusilla wanted to facepalm.

"What about you, cutie?" Lucy asked Ichabod. "What can I get you?"

Ichabod looked up at the menu and turned to Drusilla. "Any recommendations?"

She double-checked with Ichabod regarding allergies and then she ordered him a meal consisting of steak and fries with a root beer. Before walking away, Lucy gave Ichabod another smile. With a sigh, Drusilla led Ichabod to her favorite table, which was the table near the Jukebox. They both sat down, and Drusilla took a sip of her drink.

"This is great," Ichabod remarked while surveying the cafe, appreciating the decor and the handful of customers in their booths. "It's kitschy, but I like it."

"This is my favorite place to eat."

Drusilla's eyes flittered over to Lucy who was chatting with the cook and back to Ichabod, "What is your type?" She groaned and slapped her forehead. Drusilla wanted the floor to open up and swallow her.

"I–" Ichabod paused. The earlier awkwardness vanished and was replaced by an intense, hot look in his eyes that unsettled her. "I have no specific preferences when it comes to gender. Work has always been my top priority. For me, an emotional bond is necessary, but I've only felt that with a few people."

Drusilla didn't know what to say to that. She would admit to only herself that there was a big part of her that hoped the attraction between them was genuine and could lead to something more. Despite what she thought before, Ichabod has not shown any genuine interest in Katrina. Whenever Katrina was mentioned, the focus was on the horseman and other supernatural occurrences in the town.

Drusilla hoped that Ichabod's intense gaze and lingering touch were more than just friendly. Was it just Drusilla's imagination?

Drusilla trusted him before, and he had left her with a broken heart.

"Are you alright?" Ichabod asked.

"I don't–"

"Here you go, Sweetie," Lucy said, winking at Ichabod as she dropped his steak with an actual wooden stake embedded into it and fries in front of him. And then she put down Drusilla's food.

"Don't be a stranger," Lucy said.

"Are you sure you are okay?" Ichabod asked, and Drusilla gave him a strained smile.

"Peachy," Drusilla lied, finding it hard to put her emotions into words. Her life was already in shambles and Drusilla didn't want to add to it by acting on her emotions.

They spent their lunch figuring out the logistics of breaking into the church, The rest of the day was wasted searching the town archives, with no results to show for it. By the time it was dark, Drusilla's nerves were all over the place. She made Ichabod ride with her in her rental car because his car was way too inconspicuous. He grumbled about it as he tried to fit his long legs into the tiny passenger's side.

Drusilla circled the church a few times to see if she could spot Pastor Sparks's BMW, but the parking lot was empty. They parked down the street and got out of the car.

Ichabod took out a bag from the back seat and opened it up. "Here." He handed her a pair of latex gloves. "No need to leave any nasty fingerprints behind."

Drusilla sighed but took them and slid them on. They walked up to the back of the church, stopping in front of a window.

"Wait here," Ichabod said.

Drusilla opened her mouth to protest, but Ichabod quickly ran off. She huffed and hugged her arms around herself, shivering. *I'm not scared.* The temperature dropped and she left her hoodie in the car.

Eventually, Ichabod ran back to her. "No alarm." He smirked. "Lucky for us, the security in this place is terrible."

Ichabod took a crowbar out of his duffle bag, but she stopped him. "You're not going to break the glass, are you?"

He snorted and rolled his eyes. "What type of barbarian do you take me for?" Using the crowbar, he pried the window open, then bowed and waved her to the window. "After you, my lady."

Drusilla quickly climbed through the window, almost falling on her ass. She glared at Ichabod as he gracefully leaped through the window, even with a heavy duffle bag strapped to him.

"You break into places often?" Drusilla asked as they walked down the aisle.

"I'm a Paladin, remember?" Ichabod said, as he pulled out two flashlights and handed one of them to Drusilla.

"I don't think that is very Knight-like."

Ichabod snorted, "You would be surprised."

At night, the church was eerie, and it seemed that every footstep echoed as they made their way to the dais. The dim light of their flashlights barely made a dent in the darkness.

Ichabod pulled out what looked like a steampunk version of an iPod from his jacket. He plugged in his earbuds and then frowned. "There's a large amount of magic here. From the sound of it, it's a mixture of dark and white magic."

"You got all of that from an iPod?" Drusilla snorted.

"This is an Auger." Ichabod huffed, "And it picks up on inaudible vibrations, translates them to sounds that we can detect." Ichabod said as he stopped a few feet away from the dais. "There's a huge well of magic right here."

Drusilla stood beside Ichabod and tentatively knocked on the pulpit. Nothing happened. "That's where I saw the door."

"You said, the door appeared when you sang the lullaby," Ichabod reminded her. "You should try it again."

Drusilla frowned at him but then she took a deep breath and sang the song. Once again, the words came easily to Drusilla. And once again, she had to wonder if this meant that her memories were gradually returning.

Once again, the word emerged in the pulpit, and shortly after, it split apart revealing a red door, just like before.

She turned to him triumphantly. "See, I told you there was a door."

Ichabod blinked at her and then looked over to the pulpit. He frowned. "No, there isn't." Ichabod pressed his hand against the wood. "There's nothing there."

Drusilla rolled her eyes and yanked the door open, snapping her eyes closed against the sudden spill of bright white light. Strangely, she could hear the rushing of water.

"What the actual fuck?"

"Indeed," Ichabod replied dryly. "A magical portal to a temple hidden in the heart of a church? Clever."

"Temple?"

She opened her eyes and saw there beyond the door was a large chamber. It was at least three times bigger than the church itself and made of a smooth gray stone. The rush of water she'd heard came from a waterfall at the back of the chamber. What immediately caught her attention was the huge black marble statue of a woman who sat near the waterfall.

Her hands shook as Drusilla took a step forward.

Ichabod put his hands on her shoulders. She turned to look at him. "Be careful," Ichabod said. "You don't know if this portal is stable or if it'll trap you halfway across the world."

Drusilla nodded, turning back to give the portal a weary look. She could simply step back and pretend that this room didn't exist, but this place could also hold the answers they desperately needed. *For Katrina,* Drusilla thought to herself as she took a step through the door.

Drusilla took in the high vaulted ceilings, the curved benches that sat in front of beautiful arch windows, and the potted plants with their large vibrant green leaves that were dotted around the space. The place gave off an air of both reverence and peace.

"Are you okay?"

Drusilla spun around to see Ichabod still standing there. She frowned. "I'm fine, but why are you still standing there?"

Ichabod rolled his eyes. "I can't get in." He pressed against the empty air, but his hands didn't slip through the doorway. Ichabod looked at the statue and sighed. "I'll stay here and I'll be the lookout."

Drusilla bit her lip. "Are you sure?"

"Positive." Ichabod frowned. "But don't stay too long. And keep where I can see you. I don't want you to be trapped in there."

Drusilla nodded, "Okay."

She turned around and walked to the statue, her boots echoing against the colorful hexagon tiles on the floor. Golden words were written in Lonhɛian on each hexagon but she didn't stop to read any of them. She was too transfixed by the figure in front of the waterfall.

Drusilla stood in front of the statue. The woman was gorgeous. Her long locs fell to her bare shoulder. She wore a dress of golden armor, and in her hands, she held a large golden jug. Water spilled out of it and down into the fountain below.

This must be Iurti, Drusilla thought to herself as she remembered Mathilde mentioning the goddess in her dream. Curious as to what other wonders this room held, she whirled around, seeing nothing of interest and no doors leading anywhere. Her finger traced the smooth white stone of the walls but found no other hidden doors.

Drusilla sighed. "Well, this was a bust." She might as well go back before Ichabod had a fit.

She was heading back to the door when she spotted a light in the corner of the room. Cautiously tiptoeing towards it, she realized it was coming from a small, thin tube rising from the floor, on top of which was a gray hexagonal tile.

"Ichabod!" Drusilla called out. "I found something."

"What?" Ichabod said. "Drusilla—"

"Hold on!" Drusilla shouted back. There had to be a way to pull up the canisters.

Her fingers traced over the word. Usugemeu," Drusilla read out loud, and it felt just as familiar as the language from her father's lullaby. She yelped as the tile sprung from the floor, but this time, instead of a light, the canister held a scroll.

"Bloody hell," Ichabod swore under his breath.

"This isn't just a temple," Drusilla said in awe as she touched the glass and a slim opening appeared. "I think this is an archive."

Fifteen

The Wings of a Storm

"This is a lot to take in," Ichabod said, looking at all the scrolls stacked in front of them on top of the coffee table. While back at the temple, he'd given her his duffle bag, and Drusilla had stuffed as many scrolls in there as she could after taking photos of the entire temple.

Once back in the church, they'd decided to head back to Grimwood. Now, they both sat in the living room. The room was a mess of scrolls, books, and laptops.

She looked up at the grandfather clock. It was nearly eleven o'clock. Drusilla thought about starting another batch of coffee but sighed and shook her head. She picked up the scroll and noticed it was written in Lonhẽian. And just like the Magnus Test results she had found in her father's office, Drusilla had no problem reading them.

Ichabod looked down at the language and frowned. "God, I hate I can't read this. It might as well be gibberish."

"Now you know how I felt with all those Dutch journals" Drusilla shrugged. This seems like a spell that can make a person invisible.

Tapping his finger on the table, Ichabod was lost in thought. "Why all these individual scrolls? Most magicians have a book of spells."

"No luck finding a grimoire yet," Drusilla replied in frustration. "Perhaps these scrolls are meant as a form of a backup. The destruction of a grimoire can lead to the loss of an entire coven's base of knowledge."

Ichabod nodded, "You have a point."

"The place was hidden in a church. The last place you'd expect to find a treasure trove of magical knowledge."

"Your ancestors were quite clever," Ichabod said, with a rueful smile. He grabbed the scrolls and let out a tired sigh. "It will take a long time to go through all these scrolls, and it's getting late."

Drusilla heard the sound of rain hitting the windowsill. She peeked outside to see a steady deluge of rain. Turning back to Ichabod, she reluctantly said, "You better stay here for the night. Those country roads will be slick and treacherous to navigate at night."

"Thank you," Ichabod agreed. "I'll call and tell my mother I'm not making it home tonight."

I'm sure Analyn will be overjoyed, Drusilla ruefully thought to herself. She shook her head and sighed as she walked out of the living room and headed to the linen closet.

Drusilla came back with fresh sheets and blankets and handed them to Ichabod as she walked away. "The guest room's the second door on the right."

"Doctor?" Ichabod called out.

Drusilla paused but didn't dare to turn around. "Yes?"

He was silent for a long moment, but then he simply said, "Sleep well."

Drusilla shivered at the low, husky timber of his voice. A wave of arousal rushed through and pulsed between her thighs. She knew if she turned around, she might give in to the temptation. Instead, Drusilla said nothing as she hurried up the stairs into the welcome sanctuary of her bedroom.

Drusilla tried to sleep, but between her worries over her sister, her confusing feelings over Ichabod, and her recent findings, it took her some time to drift off into a fitful sleep.

Long before sunrise, she woke up with a gasp as a loud boom of thunder rocked the entire house.

Her heart was already racing from her nightmare, which replayed itself over and over in her mind. Drusilla's dreams were a tapestry of the Horseman chasing her mixed in with Saundra's brutal end. The prone body of her sister's friend had morphed into Katrina. She was met with her sister's accusing stare.

Drusilla jumped at another thunderclap, followed by the rush of heavy rain. *Well, there goes any chance of me going back to sleep*, she thought ruefully to herself as she leaned over to turn on her lamp. Drusilla frowned at her bonnet, which had fallen on the floor. She put it on the nightstand grabbed her old, tattered copy of Octavia Butler's *Kindred,* and tried to read.

Yet, no matter how hard she tried, she couldn't sink into the familiar story. With a sigh, Drusilla got out of bed, pulled on her robe and slippers, and headed downstairs.

She patted the battle horn. "God, I wish you were here, Dad. I have so many questions." Then she walked into the kitchen, eyeing the empty coffee maker.

It was too late at night for coffee and she was out of hot cocoa mix, so she just grabbed a bottle of water and sat down in the living room. Drusilla turned on the TV and flicked through a couple of channels, stopping on the History Channel. A rerun of *American Pickers* was on, and she settled down to watch Mike and Frank's shenanigans.

Drusilla heard a loud boom. She frowned, her knuckles gripping the remote in her hand. The thunder had gotten increasingly louder since she'd woken up. *How is Ichabod sleeping through all this?* She shook her head and wondered if lightning would actually strike the manor. The last time that happened, the original Van Tassel homestead had burned down.

"Oh shit!" Drusilla yelped as the floors suddenly shook. The remote clattered to the ground, and she clutched the sofa for dear life.

There was another–nearly deafening–boom, then the house stopped moving.

Panting for breath, Drusilla grabbed her chest. "What the hell was that? An earthquake in upstate New York?!"

"Drusilla!"

Drusilla darted up off the couch and spun around to see Ichabod running down the stairs and over to her. "Are you okay?"

"Yeah, I'm fine. You?" Drusilla asked, looking him over for any injuries. He looked relatively unscathed.

"I'm okay."

"What the hell *was* that?"

The house shook again, and there was another boom. Drusilla's hands instinctively covered her ears as the house trembled, causing her legs to collapse.

"It's the wards!" Ichabod said, holding on to her. "Someone's trying to break the wards."

"Wards?" Drusilla shouted, "What the fuck—"

"Someone is trying to break them!" Ichabod replied.

Drusilla groaned and slapped her forehead. Her family were witches, so of course, Grimwood had magical wards.

Ichabod scrambled to the window and all the blood drained out of his face. "Drusilla!"

She hurried over to the window just as the lighting flashed and gasped in horror.

Standing outside her house was the Headless Horseman.

Sixteen

The Thin Line

"What the fuck?" Drusilla screeched as the Horseman charged forward. Yet instead of crashing through the door, the Horseman slammed into a thin dome of energy surrounding the house.

"Oh, god he's coming," she said hysterically. "He'll get in past the wards and then he'll kill us."

"Not if you find the linchpin!" Ichabod said.

"Linchpin?" Drusilla shouted. "What the fuck is a linchpin?"

Ichabod groaned. "It's what powers the wards. It should be nearby. We just have to find it and recharge it. Once you do that, they'll be strong enough to stop him."

Drusilla's eyes darted around the room, but things were falling all over the place, and she only barely dodged a heavy tome that toppled off the closest bookshelf.

"How am I supposed to find the linchpin? And what do I do to fix it? I didn't even know about magic until three days ago!"

There was another boom, and the house shuddered again.

"I'll walk you through it," he promised. "We're dead if we don't find it."

"Thanks for the encouragement," Drusilla huffed. "What does it look like?"

"It's different for everyone," he explained, helping her sift through some of the mess on the floor. "But it'll be special to whoever put the wards up, something that has powerful meaning to them."

She took in the disaster that was her once neat and tidy living room, barely managing not to brain herself with falling objects. Her eyes darted around for something–hell, *anything*–that might be this linchpin.

And then she spotted something lying beside the turned over coffee table. It was her father's prized war horn. but she snatched it off the ground.

The moment her fingers came in contact with the horn, it began to glow with an orange light, which burst through the cracks all over the horn's surface.

"Got it!" she shouted triumphantly. "But it's breaking!"

"Try fixing it."

"How?"

"I am not the witch here," Ichabod reminded her.

Drusilla huffed and almost toppled over when there was another boom. The horn broke a bit more. Drusilla tried to call the power to her and tried to remember how it felt. But the other times she'd just acted on instinct.

The house was rocked by one last earth-shaking shudder, and the horn cracked in two.

"Oh, shit."

Suddenly, the door was ripped off its hinges, and standing in the doorway was the Horseman. In that terrifying instant, everything flooded back to her. This was the creature that had taken her sister from her, that had murdered Saundra in cold blood. Instead of being sensible, instead of being scared out of her wits, Drusilla was filled with rage that burnt red hot under her skin. Suddenly, bright orange energy flared into her hands. which she shoved on top of the two pieces of the broken horn.

Ichabod had been thrown to the ground, and he was struggling to stand up. As Drusilla watched him scrabble to his feet, time seemed to slow down. Ichabod moved like he was swimming through thick muck, and the objects falling to the floor hung in midair, dropping almost imperceptibly as the seconds ticked by. Then, everything sped up again but in reverse, Ichabod collapsing to the floor and objects zooming back up to where they'd fallen from. The horn repaired itself right in front of her eyes, clicking together and glowing brightly once more.

The Horseman was engulfed by a crackling orange energy. He struggled against it, but whatever magic was in the horn was so powerful that he fell to his knees, clutching at his chest. In a flash of blinding orange light, the Horseman was gone.

Drusilla looked around the room in awe as Ichabod hurried over to her. He kneeled beside her, taking her head in his hand. " Are you okay?"

Drusilla looked down at her hands, which were no longer glowing, and the horn, which looked like it always did: normal, innocuous, not at all like it could single-handedly banish the Horseman.

"No," Drusilla replied, her fingers trembling. "I not really okay."

Drusilla sat on the sofa clutching the war horn, muttering to herself, "This is insane." First, it was finding out her father's magical hiding spot, where she found out that both she and her sister were magically tested. Not only were her memories erased, but there was also a magical archive discovered in her old church.

An enchanted artifact that regulated the magical wards of her house was her father's most precious antique.

Drusilla should be used to this, but right now she was internally screaming.

She stared at the horn. It hadn't been her own burgeoning power or any of Ichabod's weapons that had stopped it. This horn that had sat in pride of place on the mantle for as long as she could remember had saved her.

"A linchpin," Drusilla said to herself.

"Yes," Ichabod said. "Witches attract other supernaturals, so it's not uncommon for them to put upwards in their homes to protect them."

Drusilla shook her head, "H-How do you know all this? I know you're a Paladin— "

Ichabod shook his head as he finished hammering the last of the nails into the board over the door. "We paladins work closely with witches and magicians. We have to know how magic works, even though we can't use it." He walked over to where she was sitting on the sofa, then put the hammer down on the coffee table and squatted in front of her. "Doctor?" Ichabod asked, his eyes filled with concern. "I think we should try to sleep."

Drusilla shook her head. The thought of climbing back into bed alone after everything that happened tonight terrified her, and there would be no respite for her in her dreams.

She bit her lip. "Can you stay with me? I...I don't want to be alone."

Ichabod's eyebrows rose. "Are you sure?"

Drusilla shakily got to her feet and offered him her hands. "Yes." She looked around the shattered chaos of the living room. "But not here," Ichabod smirked down at her, and Drusilla rolled her eyes. "Don't get any ideas. We're only sleeping."

"Of course," Ichabod said, his eyes dancing with mirth.

Drusilla let go of his hand and carefully made her way across the mess and then up the stairs to her bedroom. Once inside, Drusilla paused by the bed and jumped as Ichabod shut the door.

"I can go to my room," Ichabod said.

Drusilla shook her head and snatched her bonnet off the nightstand where she'd left it. "Stay," Drusilla said.

"Doctor—"

Drusilla grabbed his hand. "Please stay."

It should have stung to swallow her pride like this, but it didn't.

"Okay." Ichabod nodded, swallowing down the lump in his throat before lying down on top of the covers.

Drusilla and Ichabod stretched out awkwardly beside each other. She had so many things to say to him but she didn't know where to start. She knew she was being pathetic, just like she had been when she was eighteen. But Drusilla was so damn weak, especially when it came to Ichabod.

She listened to his breathing, felt the warmth of his skin, and caught a whiff of his musky sandalwood fragrance. "I am sorry," Drusilla said finally.

"What for?" Ichabod brushed against her. He was so close to her, but it didn't bridge the emotional gap.

"For talking to you like that at your father's funeral." Drusilla shook her head. "I was hurt, but that wasn't the time or place."

"I'm sorry too," Ichabod said. "I was so angry at you, and I lashed out."

"Is that the reason you've been an asshole to me since you came back?"

"You were just as nasty to me."

Despite apologizing and admitting he was right, Drusilla felt regretful when looking back at her actions. If Kyndall or Katrina had acted the way she did, Drusilla wouldn't hesitate to drag them for it.

"Yeah, I was," she admitted.

"Can I ask a question?"

"Okay, what?"

Ichabod gave a long sigh. "Why did you ghost me? One day we were talking and then you shut me out the next."

Drusilla blinked at him because surely Ichabod, genius extraordinaire, couldn't be this dense. "You took my virginity, and the next day, you asked Katrina to prom. She told me what you said."

"You know about that?" Ichabod immediately paled.

"Yes," Drusilla replied, angrily. "You told her that we were just friends and that you didn't see me like that the day after you fucked me." I told you I loved you and then you discarded me like trash."

Ichabod winced. "Well, that explains it."

She loved her sister, but she wasn't blind to her faults. Katrina could be a bitch, but Drusilla was grateful that her twin had come straight home and told Drusilla what Ichabod had said. It finally allowed her to see that, no matter what'd happened between them that night at the cabin, Ichabod would never love her.

"Just let it go." Drusilla looked away. While she was confident that Ichabod had moved on from her sister, she couldn't deny the undeniable chemistry between them.

Ichabod took her face into his hands, his gun-calloused fingers brushing her soft skin. Drusilla didn't have enough strength to push him away.

"Drusilla," Ichabod started and then paused. "I was a selfish, arrogant twat back then. I was so caught up in Katrina." He ruefully chuckled, "Not because I was really in love with her. I just wanted—"

She waited for him to keep going, but when he didn't, she said, "What did you want?"

He shrugged. "I never fit in anywhere. Too white to be Asian, too Asian to be white. I hated sports and would rather spend my time in books. I was the hyperactive ADHD disaster everyone picked on." He rubbed his head nervously. "Then add me being so different from what my family expected to be on top of that? I was far from being the son my father wanted."

Drusilla winced, remembering all the loud fights between Ichabod and his father.

"There is no excuse for what I did to you. Back then, I was more in love with what Katrina represented than who she really was." He shook his head, "But when you kissed me, I was terrified at how much I loved you. You and my mother were one of the few stable things in my life and it scared me to lose you."

"But what about what you said to Katrina?"

"I ridiculously thought being with Katrina could make my feelings go away." Ichabod shook his head. "I was a fool. No matter how hard I tried, I couldn't stop loving you."

"Don't." Drusilla put her hand over his mouth. "Don't say that if you don't mean it." She took a deep, shuddering breath. "You said you didn't feel that way about me."

Ichabod took her hand from his mouth and kissed her knuckles. "I was lying to myself. There hasn't been a day since I left this town that you haven't been in my thoughts. No matter how I tried, I couldn't escape you."

"Then why the attitude? Why have you been such an asshole?"

"You abandoned me during the worst time of my life, and I was so angry for so long. The one person who I needed the most, and you just shut me out of your life," Ichabod said. "But now that I know Katrina told you everything? I don't even blame you."

"Ichabod…"

Drusilla knew she should stop, should make him leave, but she was so goddamn tired of fighting. She closed the scant inches between them and pressed her lips to his.

Seventeen

A Sudden Key

Her blood was like fire, and she thrummed from the feel of his hard body pressed against hers as he took her mouth in a long, hard kiss. That hot, wet tongue--often used to recite poetry and rant about horror films and historical inaccuracies–was wicked indeed as it delved into her mouth.

Drusilla wouldn't let him get his way that easily, and her tongue dueled back for dominance as her hands slipped through his hair. A part of her missed his long hair. It was much too short now. Drusilla remembered the one and only time she'd had the privilege of running her fingers through it, the way it'd felt in her hands, the way it'd tickled her thighs as he–.

Ichabod pulled her closer until she was practically sitting in his lap, his hard cock pressed up against her throbbing center. She wanted him. No, *needed* him. Drusilla broke the kiss, throwing her head back at the delicious friction of their bodies.

"C-clothes...off," Drusilla gasped, shivering as he drew his teeth across her neck.

"Ladies first," he said, his voice low and husky.

She shuddered in his arms as he tugged her pajama top over her head, his hands immediately going to her breasts. His rough fingers swiped across her erect nipples. Drusilla jumped as he pinched them.

"Shit," Ichabod swore as he took both breasts in his hands and squeezed them.

He dipped down and took her nipple into his mouth. Drusilla bucked against him, relishing his tongue lapping against her nipple, his beard tickling against the underside of her breasts. He squeezed her other breast, his dexterous fingers flicking and twisting the sensitive bud.

Drusilla groaned and threw her head back at the dual sensations, the bit of pain mixed in with pleasure. After what seemed like an age, he released her breast with an obscene pop and repeated his sinful torture on her other breast.

All Drusilla could do was hold his head to her breasts. She was so wet that it soaked her pajama bottoms through.

"Please..." Drusilla couldn't help the whimper.

He was only playing with her breasts, and Drusilla didn't know how she was going to feel when he finally entered her. She shivered at the thought. Memories from their first time in that cabin flooded her mind. Ichabod was no longer that teenage boy. He was a man with what she assumed was years of experience, and she ached for him.

Drusilla pushed away from him and shoved down her pajama pants. She threw across the room, "Fuck me!"

He looked up, his eyes so dark they were like black holes sucking her in. He smirked. "As you wish."

Ichabod quickly got out of his shirt and pants, almost tripping over his own feet to get out of his boots. She practically melted at the sight of his naked body. He was lean and muscular, and his skin was a road map of scars. Her inner medical examiner kicked in as she cataloged the knife scars, burns, and–Jesus, were those large *claw marks* spanning the width of his torso? *How is he even alive right now?* Drusilla thought to herself, but then she quickly got distracted by his cock.

Ichabod's thick, erect member fascinated Drusilla. It wasn't particularly long, but what it lacked in length, it absolutely made up for in girth. Her pussy clenched in anticipation of having all that inside of her.

"I have condoms in the drawer," she told him.

Ichabod's eyes went wide, but he hurried to the nightstand. Inside there was an assortment of dildos and vibrators of many colors, textures, and sizes.

"You keep busy, I see."

Drusilla snorted. "I'm single, not a monk."

"Oh, treasure," Ichabod said as he took out a purple vibrator shaped like a dick with an attachment for clit play. "I'm going to have so much fun with these later."

Drusilla's hands dipped between her legs, and she parted them wide so Ichabod could get a full view of her pussy. Her fingers spread her lips apart, and with her free hand, she rubbed her throbbing clit. She jerked her hips back. She was so turned on right now that it was almost too much.

Ichabod froze. "Are you trying to kill me, woman?" Ichabod grabbed a condom and hurried back over to her.

Drusilla sat up and shoved him back on the bed. It was now Ichabod that was spread naked against her sheets. She snatched the condom and tore it open. "Don't you dare move!" Then Drusilla slid the condom over the head of his cock. Ichabod groaned and twitched. Drusilla smirked and gazed at him through her lashes. wrapping her fingers around the base of her prize. She tightened her grip around his member and used her mouth to slide the condom down his cock. Once she was done, she gave one last lingering lick at the underside of Ichabod's length. He jerked in her grip before she finally released him with a *pop*.

Ichabod moaned at the loss in her mouth. But she wouldn't disappoint him for too long. She straddled his hips, already so wet that she could slip down his cock with ease. Drusilla slapped her hands on his chest, a cry leaving her mouth at the feeling of Ichabod filling her.

"Oh, fuck," he swore, his hips jerking. "Ride me, darling."

Drusilla pushed back her curls and slid all the way up his cock until the tip was almost out, then slammed down hard. Ichabod arched into it, whimpering and gasping as she took her pleasure from him. His hips jerked up to meet her, thrust after delicious thrust, and they fell into a slow rhythm. The desperation she'd been feeling faded into the back of her mind.

Drusilla rode him slow and hard, bouncing up and down on his cock. All Ichabod could do at first was take what she gave him. But he wasn't one to lie idle for too long, and soon he was sitting up, his face firmly in between her breasts as he bucked up inside her over and over again. His movements were hard, and punishing. The new angle directly hit her sweet spot. Drusilla's mouth fell open, and she gripped the sides of his head, pressing him into her chest. Then the bastard reached between a hand between the two of them to rub her pulsing clit.

Once, twice, three times and Drusilla's whole body was shuddering from the force of her orgasm.

Drusilla slumped against him, and Ichabod kissed her again before he laid her down on her back and slammed right back into her. He moaned and gripped her hips so hard, she wouldn't be surprised if he left bruises.

He slid in and out of her in quick strokes, chasing his pleasure now that she'd gotten her own. Drusilla's hands ran down his sweat-slicken back, her exhausted body rocking into him.

"Ichabod!" Drusilla called out.

"Say it again," Ichabod growled, his eyes fierce and dark with pleasure. "Say my name!"

"Ichabod!"

He slammed into her once, twice, and a third time before he finally came. And goddamn, this man was beautiful when he finally let go of that stiff British upper lip. She reached up and jerked his head down to lick into his lips.

Ichabod moaned into her mouth, then slumped down on top of her. They lay like that, panting for breath, the scent of sex wafting heavily in the air.

"Stay right there," he said.

Ichabod stood up and stretched. Unbothered by his own nudity, he padded out of the room. Drusilla lay there, her mind a muddled mess and too tired to think about what this meant. Moments later, Ichabod came back in and sat down next to her.

"Lay still, love," he murmured. After dropping the soiled duvet off the bed, Ichabod slid between the cool sheets and gathered her close.

Drusilla knew she could resist–*should* resist–but it was too late for regrets. Those could wait until morning.

With a sigh, she laid her head on top of his chest. His hand rubbed up and down her nude skin, leaving goosebumps in his wake. The silence was comfortable, the words that needed to be said quieted for the moment, and Drusilla closed her eyes and let sleep take her.

Drusilla gasped as she woke up. Her eyes darted around the room but she was no longer in the grips of the Horseman but in her warm comfortable bed. Ichabod was pressed against her back, his nose buried in her hair, which had to be a tangled, wild mess because she'd forgotten her bonnet. His hands wrapped around her waist and his breath tickled the back of her neck. Drusilla longed to bask in the comfort of his presence as her smaller hands pressed against his larger ones.

When Ichabod left Sleepy Hollow sixteen years ago, Drusilla thought she would never have this again. She wanted to hold on to her earlier happiness but her nightmares tainted it. *When will this be over?* Drusilla thought to herself in frustration.

These nightmares had been a constant in Drusilla's life for as long as she could remember, and she was sick of it. The dreams served as a reminder that Katrina was at the mercy of the Horseman. Despite everything, she believed that her sister was still alive. Drusilla was a logical person, but she knew deep in her heart she would have felt the splintering of their bond.

She couldn't stop reliving the nightmare in her mind. Mathilde's horse ride through the town, the chase through the woods, their confrontation with the Horseman through the woods, and finally the trap that Mathilde's coven had sprung.

Drusilla struggled to think of any other clues aside from the prophecy that could be of use. *Maybe I missed something?* Drusilla pondered the details in her mind.

But there was nothing new.

Drusilla gave a defeated sigh.

She managed to untangle herself from Ichabod. Drusilla needed a shower and a cup of coffee asap. Then something occurred to her: there was something familiar about that clearing.

Her mind immediately went back to the book she read in the library when she saw the illustration of Major Andre hanging from a tulip tree with a heart-shaped knot in the bark.

"SHIT!"

Drusilla hurried out of bed and dressed. Ichabod groaned and sat up, his hair all over the place.

"Love, what's wrong?"

Drusilla turned around, her eyes wide. "I know how to find the Horseman's head."

Ichabod's eyes narrowed in confusion. "What? But he doesn't have one."

"Yes," Drusilla said. "And I have a hunch that this is how the Horseman was resurrected. If we destroy the head—"

"We can destroy the Horseman." Ichabod finished. "But how do we find it? It can be anywhere."

"Lucky for you," Drusilla smirked, "I know where to find it."

"How?"

Drusilla gripped his arms. All along, the dreams were pointing toward the Head's location. "If we follow Mathilde's route, we can find the head."

"And you think his head is still where they left it?"

"Only one way to find out."

She hurried over to her phone and plotted each landmark Mathilde had shown her into her maps app, then shoved her phone in Ichabod's face.

Ichabod took her into his arms and kissed her softly. "Brilliant, absolutely brilliant!"

For the first time in longer than she cared to admit, Drusilla laughed. "None of that. We got work to do."

Eighteen

Heads Will Roll

"I think we're lost," Ichabod huffed as he sat down on top of a large, flat rock.

Drusilla studied the map on her phone. They had dutifully followed Mathilde's trail, going past the gristmill and the Old Dutch Church, then across the red covered bridge into the forest. She'd thought that her connection to her ancestor would easily lead her to the tulip tree, but now she wasn't so sure.

The morning quickly passed into the frigid afternoon. Drusilla and Ichabod ate a quick packed lunch and got back to their search. They spent hours trudging through the forest, which just reinforced Drusilla's deep hatred of hiking. *If I see never another tree again, it will be too soon*, Drusilla thought to herself as she checked the map on her phone.

Drusilla was thankful that she'd had the foresight to download it to her phone because the reception here was crap. The longer they were in the forest, the more foolish she felt. Drusilla had naively hoped that her mystical connection to Mathilde would lead to her to the horseman's head.

Drusilla nearly tripped over a root and swore under her breath.

"Are you alright?" Ichabod asked as he hurried over to her.

Drusilla put her hand up. "I'm fine." She threw a suspicious look at the nearby fallen tree and sighed. "But I think we walked past that log at least five times." She rubbed her forehead. "We're going around in circles."

Drusilla walked over to the tree and sat down on it, putting her head in her hands. They needed to find both the head and Katrina. Drusilla and Ichabod had already wasted enough time as it was.

She could hear the crunch of leaves under Ichabod's heavy footsteps. Suddenly, he pulled her in and wrapped his arms around her.

"What the hell are we supposed to do?" Drusilla grumbled. "I can't even find one goddamn tree."

He dropped a kiss on top of her head. "We'll find it, you'll see."

Drusilla sat there for a long moment before she finally looked up at the sky. It was no longer blue; the clouds were soft pink with orange hues. The trees were beautiful, the orange, red, gold, and brown leaves swaying in the breeze.

"We wasted enough time" Drusilla muttered. "Katrina's missing, and I'm off on some wild goose chase. What if this doesn't work? What if–"

"You're being too hard on yourself, love."

Drusilla's heart skipped a beat. This was the second time he'd called her "love," It was so bizarre given they'd only slept together once since he'd come back. Although they had a heart to heart talk and fantastic sex, their relationship wasn't permanent.

Katrina is in danger now. Think about your fucked up love life later, she scolded herself.

Drusilla coughed and stood up. "We should get going."

Ichabod checked his watch. "Yeah, it's getting late."

Drusilla and Ichabod headed off again, not really talking much. The closer it got to dark, the worse she felt about her decision to come out there. Despite being a rational adult, she allowed herself to be consumed by all this magical nonsense. *This is not helping Katrina.*

Ichabod put a hand out to stop her, "Do you hear that?"

Drusilla paused to listen, "I don't hear–"

It was faint, so faint that Drusilla could miss it but it sounded like whimpering.

"Hello?" Drusilla called out.

Ichabod stepped in front of her, gun at the ready as they followed the sound through trees. The closer they got, the more that Drusilla could hear that it was a person sobbing. "Hello? Do you need help?"

The sobbing suddenly stopped and there was a weak familiar voice. "Drusilla?"

Ichabod shouted Drusilla's name as she broke into a run and could hear him running after her. She abruptly pushed beyond a corpse of trees and into a clearing. Other side of it, near the edge, was Katrina tied to the tulip tree.

"Drusilla!" Katrina cried out as she struggled against her bonds. "It really is you!"

Drusilla hurried to her sister, her eyes going wide as she saw Katrina's injuries. Her skin was a canvas of deep cuts and bruises. Drusilla went to untie her and jerked back in surprise, "You're freezing!"

She turned to Ichabod. "Katrina needs medical attention. I have to check her more thoroughly, but it's way too cold out here. The Horseman must've been stashing her somewhere else because she doesn't have frostbite, thank god."

A strange look crossed Ichabod's face, but he quickly took off his coat and handed it to Drusilla.

"Ichabod— "Katrina shook her head. "What?" She threw a confused look at her sister.

Drusilla gave her sister a wry smile, "Don't worry! He's here to help us." She finished untying Katrina and helped her stand. Her sister wavered unsteadily for a moment.

"Can you walk?" Drusilla asked.

Yeah, I think I can make it." Katrina nodded. "You actually came for me."

"You are my sister," Drusilla said, "I wasn't going to let you go out like that."

Ichabod coughed, "Ladies, as endearing as this is. I think we should go."

Abruptly, they all froze as they heard the loud sounds of hooves.

"It's the Horseman!" Katrina screamed.

"Are you kidding me right now?" Drusilla said. "Your gun didn't do anything last time."

"Take Katrina and run!" Ichabod ordered.

"The last time I checked, we are the only ones who have powers."

"Katrina still got taken hostage," Ichabod pointed out. "And your powers aren't all that reliable."

Ichabod charged forward and started firing at the horseman. Besides, Katrina needed to get to a hospital. Katrina started to pull Drusilla away. Her sister needed to get to the hospital but Drusilla couldn't just leave Ichabod.

She wrenched out of Katrina's grasp and turned back. Time seemed to slow down as she watched the Horseman gallop towards Ichabod, using his ax to slice Ichabod's hand off at the wrist before severing his head in one quick movement.

Drusilla cried out as his body dropped to the ground next to his severed head and hand.

"Juodbrarle," Katrina said.

In her grief, Drusilla had almost forgotten her sister was there. She tried to turn to Katrina to tell her to run, but her body was frozen. She couldn't move. Was Drusilla going into some type of shock?

Katrina walked around to face her.

"Ridta gærbɛ̃m," Katrina said, and with a swipe of her hand across her body, her injuries disappeared and her dress was repaired. She looked like she'd just walked out of a church committee meeting.

"You know what your problem is?" Katrina said, wagging her finger at Drusilla like she was a naughty child. "You could never mind your own fucking business."

And then, with another quick whisper of a word, Drusilla was falling onto the ground.

The last thing Drusilla saw was Ichabod's lifeless hazel eyes staring back at her.

Nineteen

The Cost of Vengeance

Awareness came back to Drusilla slowly. Her body felt heavy and weary. She wanted to go back to sleep, but something kept nagging at her. Someone was breathing heavily in her ears. Drusilla tried to scoot away from the annoyance, wanting to tell whoever it was to shut up so she could finally sleep, but Drusilla couldn't speak.

A shiver went down her spine. Her brain was fuzzy, but deep down, Drusilla knew something was wrong. With considerable effort, she pried her eyes open.

The full moon hung over the dark sky. Drusilla's heart pounded in her chest as she tried to move but couldn't. Her hands and feet were tied with rope. And there was someone so close to her she could feel their body heat, but she could only make out a peek of short hair and pale skin.

Bile rose in her throat as she spotted Ichabod's headless body. His head had rolled away, but his severed hand was near him, still grasping his gun.

Suddenly, there was a heavy crunch of boots. Then, she was jerked into a sitting position. Drusilla screamed as she noticed the Horseman looming over her.

"Now that you have a good front-row seat," Katrina sneered, finally coming into view, "let's get on with the main event." She looked like a veritable stranger standing there in the moonlight, clutching hold of the Horseman's head with one hand and what looked like the family bible in the other hand.

Drusilla could now see another man lying only a few feet from her. The Horseman jerked the man up, and she could see his face.

It was Pastor Sparks.

His eyes were round, and his face was ghostly pale as the tree the Horseman was dragging him to. The Horseman yanked Pastor Sparks to the white tree.

Katrina tucked the Horseman's head under her elbow, then walked to Pastor Sparks. ""Cre dazeu," She said, and pointed to Pastor Sparks. An azure color energy hit him in the chest.

Pastor Sparks gasped and coughed. "What did you do to me, you crazy bitch?"

"A truth spell." Katrina jerked his chin up and smirked down at him. "And I only have one, singular question for you, so if you are a good boy and answer truthfully, you get to die quickly."

"You're not going to get away with this, you—" He stopped as his eyes landed on Drusilla. "Are you going to just sit here?" Pastor Sparks demanded.

Drusilla tried to plead with Katrina to stop it, tried to reason with her, but nothing made it past her lips.

"Cut off his leg," Katrina said, stepping back. The Horseman moved forward, bringing the ax down on his leg. Blood splattered all over the Horseman's already filthy attire.

Pastor Sparks screamed as tears streamed down his face. But he didn't move. He was as still as a statue as he screamed into the night.

Katrina grabbed his hair and pulled his head back. "My sister can't help you. No one can help you."

Drusilla could only stare at the stranger wearing her sister's face. Because no matter how deep the chasm between them, she was still family. This was her sister, the one she used to play Barbies with, who'd crept into her bed at night when her parents fought, and who used to adopt every stray animal she came across.

Sometimes while she hadn't been paying attention over the years, Katrina had turned into a monster, one who watched calmly as the creature she'd summoned killed her own friends and now calmly ordered the torture of another.

"Ah, why the long face?" Katrina taunted. "It's not like the good pastor didn't deserve it."

Drusilla just glared back, tears stinging her eyes.

"You are such a pain in my ass." Katrina shook her head. " You got a little power and now you are feeling yourself. Newsflash, big sis? You ain't shit compared to me."

"You have already killed three people, "Drusilla felt ill as she stared at her Katrina. Her sister's typical brown eyes were glowing a bright electric blue. "Your pet monster killed Ichabod!"

"Ooh poor Ichabod," Katrina mocked her and then sneered. "You are so pathetic. He was a Paladin and they are here to do The Conclave's dirty work. Ichabod was just using you to get to me."

"No," Drusilla denied, her stinging with unshed tears. "He wouldn't do that." If this was high school Ichabod, Drusilla might have believed it. However, Drusilla could see how much Ichabod has grown since then. Although Ichabod never committed to staying permanently, Katrina's description of him was a stark contrast to the man she had come to know over the past week.

"You are so naive Dru," Katrina rolled her eyes. "I have been watching you all week. I saw you in my scrying bowl following Crane around like a bitch in heat. It's really pathetic."

"Fuck you, Katrina!" Drusilla snarled, as struggled against her bonds. She wanted to slap that smug ass smirk off her sister's face.

"Oh, you can't be mad about the paladin." Katrina shook her head. "Honestly, I did you a favor." It seemed like Katrina's humanity had largely vanished after Brom's death. Katrina was taking revenge for her lost love by stealing Drusilla's.

Drusilla had lost so much: first her mother, then her father, then Ichabod. And now her sister was gone, too, lost in the darkness of rage and grief.

For the first time in her life, Drusilla was truly alone.

"Now, back to our little game," Katrina said, as she turned back to Pastor Sparks. "Randy, I know you and your little friends murdered my Brom."

"No, we loved Brom!"

"Cut off the other leg," Katrina ordered, and the Horseman quickly obeyed.

Pastor Sparks flopped onto the ground, his screams rending through the chilly night air.

Katrina smirked at him. "You loved Brom? You loved Brom so much that you, Denis, and Saundra loured him to the cabin, shot him, and left him for dead. You even had the fucking audacity to come to Brom's funeral, to give your condolences, and pretend that you were my fucking friends.

"You thought you were so smart," she said coldly. "And if that half-wit of a sheriff had actually done an investigation, you'd already be in prison. You left so many clues behind, but the calls from Saundra? The way that your phone GPS pinged you near Brom's cabin. How about the fight you, Denis, and Brom had a few weeks before his murder? But there is one question I have for you.

"Wh-what?"

"Why?" Katrina. "I want to know why you lured him into that cabin. I want to know why you killed him."

Drusilla didn't know what to think. Her mind immediately went back to that police report she had found. Brom, Denis, and Pastor Sparks had gotten into a fight and it had been so serious that deputies had to break it up.

"I don't know what—"

"Wrong answer." She turned to the Horseman. "Cut off the other arm."

Drusilla looked away. She still heard the pastor's anguished cries.

"WHY?!?" Katrina demanded.

"Fine! You want the truth!" Pastor Sparks shouted. "Your precious Brom was fucking my wife and Saundra. Hell, the bastard practically fucked anything that moved."

"No, Brom wouldn't do that to me!"

"You thought everything was a fairytale but Brom was far from being Prince Charming!"

The Horseman suddenly jerked into motion. One moment, Pastor Sparks was ranting, and then next, with a loud thud, his head was rolling onto the ground.

Katrina spun on the Horseman. "I didn't tell you to kill him yet."

The Horseman ignored her and turned to Drusilla.

"Wait!" Katrina said, her eyes glowing with a bright blue energy.

The Horseman froze.

Katrina held the Horseman's head aloft by its hair, waving it around. "I am your master, and you have to do what I say."

The Horseman walked back over to his mistress, but instead of stopping, he simply snatched his head out of her hands and shoved it into a nearby tree.

With his head in one hand and his ax in the other, the Horseman turned around and stalked towards Drusilla.

Twenty

Intertwined and Apart

The ax fell, and Drusilla rolled away as quickly as she could, but she still cried out when she felt a sharp pain in her arm.

"I said stop!" Katrina said, her hands glowing with magic.

The Horseman swung again, but a blue energy shield met his ax, crackling like electricity.

Katrina crawled over to the family bible, or what it really was: the family grimoire. This is why Katrina had wanted it so badly.

Drusilla struggled against her rope, and with enough pressure, the rope broke, but the force field vanished.

"Vieua," Katrina read from the bible and the Horseman lunged but froze mid-swing.

The Horseman lunged again but froze mid-swing. Heart pounding in her chest, Drusilla witnessed Katrina snatch the Horseman's head back and lift it into the air.

"You are under my command," Katrina sneered at the Horseman.

Drusilla sighed. "This has to be your worst plan."

"Shut up," Katrina replied, curtly. "I'm trying to save your life."

Drusilla tried to access the power inside of her, desperate to show her sister how "common" she really was, but her magic was so unreliable. It was obvious she had none of Katrina's expertise with it.

Katrina huffed and walked over to the Horseman, raising her free hand, the energy hovering and cycling around her palm. Drusilla used her sister's distraction to untie her hands and feet. Her eyes went back to Ichabod's body and then to Katrina.

"I don't need you anymore, for now," Katrina said as she flipped through the family grimoire, which Drusilla realized was the bible.

"Here it is! The banishing spell." She put her free hand next to the Horseman's head. "Delme bierme elementse stende plon avna—"

Suddenly, the Horseman lurched forward so hard that it knocked Katrina to the ground. Once again, the Horseman's head tumbled from her grasp and rolled several feet away from her.

Katrina put her hands up, power blasting through her fingertips, but this time, the Horseman walked past the shield with ease. His ax hit true, slicing into her stomach. Katrina grasped her abdomen. Blood poured from the wound, quickly staining her hands and her pretty sundress with crimson.

Drusilla shot to her feet, as she ran for the head. Her eyes darted to the grimore that uselessly next to a prone Katrina. The spell had sound very familiar. It was the spell that Mathlide's spell. And lucky for her, she could clearly remember the words.

Delme bierme elementse stende plon avna,
te e aide bierme horseman s oso,
suande atme, nuf, plin e frue—

The Horseman spun on his feet and rushed her.

"Drusilla!" Katrina shouted, and suddenly there was power rushing through her body.

The fire of her own power mingled and consumed all all of Katrina's ice cold power. The surge was immense and more overwhelming than her earlier experiences with magic. Drusilla felt like she was a cup about to overflow. And suddenly memories flashed before her eyes. Her father teaching her first spell, the magical games she used to play with Katrina, and her treasured memory of her father reading bible verses was replaced with him Drusilla sitting on his knee with the grimore in her father's hand as he taught her about Iurti, their creator and the magical language she had bestowed on on them. Her birthright and the magical language of her ancestors.

"*Bierme nu s voin does cuin falter bierme angique slides mue,*

bierme freunde is sprunge,
suande these uordse uepre ien crin

Drusilla felt like she was watching the entire moment outside of herself. The Horseman's eyes glowed an eerie, bright red color as both its head and its nearby body quickly shattered into pieces and burst into flame before dissolving into ash. What was left of the head slipped through her fingers and fell to the ground. Katrina coughed.

"Katrina!"

Drusilla tore off her jacket and took off her t-shirt, leaving her only in a tank top. She brushed Katrina's fingers away and staunched the blood. If Katrina didn't get to a hospital soon, she would die.

Katrina chuckled. "I don't know why you're helping me."

Drusilla glared at Katrina. "You're my sister, and you're not allowed to fucking die."

Katrina rolled her eyes. "Just heal me."

Drusilla stopped what she was doing and looked at her sister, "Heal? I don't know—"

"There is a goddamn Grimore sitting right there," Katrina gritted out. "Look it up!"

Drusilla flipped her off, "Don't get smart with me. You lucky I am saving you at all." She ran over to the grimoire and picked up. If the situation hadn't been so dire, Drusilla would have loved to spend hours combing over it. Unfortunately, there was no time to waste. *Where is it,* Drusilla thought to herself as frantically flipped through the old thick sepia brown parchment pages until she found a page that with the title Healing Spell. "Found it!"

Katrina just glared at her, but it was hard to take her as a serious threat when she was bleeding out on the forest floor.

Drusilla put her hands over the injury and repeated, "Oin uea onrteu."

The wound began to heal, as if she were watching the wound happen in reverse.

Katrina gasped, her body arching against the power before she fell unconscious. Drusilla noticed where her broken rope led, and quickly tied Katrina's hands with the smaller pieces of rope. It wasn't much, but it would do for now.

Drusilla stood up, and the magic inside her seemed to crackle under her skin. She turned and saw Ichabod. Drusilla flipped through the pages of the grimoire until she found a spell that could bring a person back from the brink of death.

Drusilla had all of this power inside of her and if magic could heal her sister. It was a long shot, but maybe, just maybe, magic could bring Ichabod back to her.

She hurried over to Ichabod's body. She quickly gathered together his severed head and arm. Drusilla quickly pieced Ichabod together like a puzzle, muttering the spell and re-knitting his head and arm to his body.

"Huŕ wẽ yẽn," she chanted, putting her hands over his chest and trying to pour as much magic into him as she could.

Drusilla fervently hoped that she could bring her love back. The magic soaked into Ichabod's body like a sponge, but nothing happened.

Drusilla wasn't a religious person. She hadn't been in a church in years, but she remembered Mathilde talk of the Great Mother and the statue in the temple.

"Please, Iurti. Please help me, please bring him back to me."

Nothing happened.

Drusilla slumped down on top of Ichabod's body and sobbed. After everything that had happened, after all their years of separation, she thought maybe they could figure things out. But he'd been taken from her again, and even with her body bubbling over with power, she still couldn't bring back the man she loved.

I didn't get a chance to tell him I loved him, Drusilla thought to herself.

They'd both wasted all that time just for her to lose him again. Drusilla stiffened, feeling like someone was watching her.

Drusilla looked up, and there in the brilliant light was a beautiful Black woman with deep ebony skin, so dark it was practically shining in the moonlight.

She knew deep in her heart that it was Iurti.

Drusilla could only stare as Iurti traced a symbol on Ichabod's forehead, and it glowed a bright, golden yellow before it finally faded. Drusilla gasped as his body suddenly seized and arched off the ground before he coughed.

His beautiful hazel eyes opened, and Drusilla's lips met his. Ichabod's kiss sang through her veins. He moaned against her, and Drusilla thought she could spend the rest of her life kissing him.

"What's the matter?" His fingers came up to brush her tears from her cheeks.

"I-I love you," Drusilla said. "I love you so damn much."

Ichabod's mouth split into a wide grin, and he kissed her again, long and hard. "I love you, too."

They pressed their heads together and just soaked up each other's presence.

Eventually, Ichabod pulled away from and gazed around the clearing. "Where is the Horseman, why is Katrina tied up, and is that Pastor Sparks? What in the bloody hell is going on here?"

Drusilla looked up, and she remembered Iurti, who had disappeared sometime during their tearful reunion.

I'll make sure to leave an offering soon, Drusilla promised herself.

"The Horseman is dead," Drusilla said as stared at her sister. Katrina's power still bubbled inside of her. "and the rest is a very long story."

Epilogue

Drusilla wrapped her scarf around her neck, shivering under the frigid air. She looked down at the bouquet of primroses and hellebores that was in her hands   Ichabod wrapped an arm around her and pulled her close. She soaked in the comforting warmth of his body. Her ear was pressed against his chest.

It had been a few weeks since Ichabod's temporary death, and she'd taken every chance she got to reassure herself that Ichabod was still alive.

He kissed her on her forehead. "Are you sure? I don't want to intrude."

"Yes." Drusilla sighed and straightened up. "I want you there."

Ichabod laced their fingers together. "After you, treasure."

Drusilla wanted to roll her eyes, but her mouth quirked into a small smile as they walked up to the wrought-iron gates of Sleepy Hollow Cemetery. She slipped her hand in his as they treaded through the snow to the large, gray tombstone near where the cemetery met the woods.

Drusilla brushed away the snow, and the words "Baltus Van Tassel 1971-2023" were engraved on his headstone.

"Dad, I bought some of your favorites from the greenhouse." She laid them carefully on the grave.

Drusilla smiled wistfully as she remembered how excited her father had been when he finally put in the greenhouse.

"I know it's been a while since I've been here," Drusilla said as she stood. "I could give you an excuse, but the truth is..." Drusilla let out a deep breath, her eyes stinging with tears. Ichabod squeezed her hand, and she continued, "It's been really hard here without you. It's been so difficult to keep the family together. You asked me to look after Katrina and–" Drusilla paused before speaking again, "I tried my best, but Katrina isn't right. Hasn't been right in a long time."

She sighed and wiped away tears, taking comfort from Ichabod beside her.

"Katrina's done a lot of messed up things," Drusilla continued, "Things that I can't forgive her. We are both going to get help. The one of the few good things that came from all of this is I needed therapy."

Drusilla knew her father wouldn't be happy with her. "We keep things in the family," Baltus had always said. Drusilla had tried therapy before, expecting it to be some instant cure her of grief but she had been wrong.

She learned that overcoming grief was a lengthy process. Denis, Saundra, and Pastor Sparks could have been alive today if Katrina had received the helped she needed.

Sending Katrina to a mental health facility in another state was the only choice she had. After a heated argument, Drusilla and Ichabod had both decided that prison (either magical or common) wasn't the best place for her sister. As for the evidence and clean up? Well, with a whispered spell or two. They made it look like Pastor Sparks was the Horseman.

Even Katrina had murdered him, Ichabod had lied to The Conclave and helped cover up for her.

"I'm not doing it for her," Ichabod had insisted. "I'm doing this for you."

It wasn't anything close to justice, but it would have to do.

Consequently, Drusilla was now the Tiraunt of Sleepy Hollow. Although she was the last Van Tassel witch and had no coven, she was still responsible for safeguarding the area.

The last few weeks were spent by Drusilla playing catch up and honing her new power. Her progress was faster than expected thanks to her restored memories.

"You may not agree with what I did, but you kept things from me, too. You had my memories erased, you kept my magic and our family history from me. So I have to do the best thing for myself. I'm so angry at you, and I don't understand why you did what you did." Drusilla took a deep breath. "I love you, but I got to live for me now."

She turned away, and together, Ichabod and Drusilla walked silently back through the quiet cemetery.

"The Horseman's gone, and your mother is safe," Drusilla finally said after a while. "Where are you off to now?"

Ichabod stopped and gave her a surprised look. "I'm not going anywhere."

"What?"

"You are a new Tiraunt," Ichabod said. "And think that you are going to need the help with your new territory."

"Yeah," Drusilla agreed. In the supernatural realm, Drusilla was a newcomer and needed all the help she could get. Despite this, she remained disappointed. *At least he staying, even if he's not staying for me.*

Ichabod continued, "Besides, the university offered me a full-time position"

Drusilla attempted to smile, but her feelings got the best of her. Analyn was going to be thrilled to have her son back home for good.

He took her face in his hands as he brought her close. "I love you so much, Drusilla, and I will not waste this second chance. I can't deny it anymore, you're the one for me."

Drusilla leaned up and pressed her lips against his. He sighed as he kissed her slowly and tenderly right there in the middle of the cemetery. They finally broke apart, and she smiled up at him.

"I love you too," she replied with a soft smile.

And together, Drusilla and Ichabod walked away from their grief and sadness into a new life.

Bonus Chapter

Drusilla put a finger to his lips to stop him. "This is wonderful, thank you." She replaced her finger with her mouth and kissed him slowly. Ichabod groaned as their mouths moved over each other. He pulled her close and Drusilla groaned as she felt his hard length pressed against her through his pants.

Ichabod's tongue danced against hers, and Drusilla wrapped her arms around him as she ground her hips against his aching need. Ichabod broke apart and pressed his head to hers. "Treasure, you are such a delightful temptation."

Drusilla laughed huskily, "Well, can I tempt you to fuck me, Mr. Crane?"

Become A Patron And Get Instant Access To This Bonus Chapter!

Acknowledgements

This book would not be here if it wasn't for all the ichabbie stans that have been cheering me on. From the moment I pitched the initial concept to publication, your enthusiasm and your unflinching belief that I could finish this book have been the motivation that kept me going for the two and half years that it took to publish this book. Thank you so much! I also want to thank all of my beta readers who gave me such valuable feedback, especially in the early stages of writing books.

I would also be remiss if I didn't mention my Filipino sensitivity readers P.K. Reeves and Cat Giarldo really came through for me and Ichabod would have been lackluster without their input. And finally, I want to thank my editors Ivy Quinn and Gabriel Hargrave. You both took my book to the next level and really made it shine.

Thank you so much for going above and beyond for me! I am so grateful to have your expertise and support.

About the Author

Georgina Kiersten (Japser Hyde/Rian Fox) is a Black non-binary author who was raised in San Antonio, Texas. Living with a disability has given Georgina the ability to see the world in a unique and open way that shines through their writing. When they not writing and reading the latest books, Georgina is a graphic designer by trade and a bit of a geek. They also juggle the humongous task of raising five kids and their horde of cats and dogs.

https://twitter.com/ingloriousgigi

tiktok.com/@ingloriousgigi

instagram.com/ingloriousgigi

facebook.com/ingloriousgigi

goodreads.com/author/show/42292661.Jasper_Hyde

THE MAGNFICIENT ENGINE

Black-centered LGBTQ+ romance.

GEORGINA KIERSTEN

Fall Into You

In Appeley, for the first time ever, Imari feels welcome, happy, and unapologetically herself. She tries new things, makes brand-new friends and, while attending the fall apple festival, she accidentally bumps into a very familiar face...

Cassidy Martinez was her childhood best friend and partner in crime. Now, she has grown into a stunning, confident woman, and Imari can't help noticing.

Should she take a risk?

More to Love

Recent divorcé, Emmy Park was content to only experience romance from his favorite Austen novels. But when a lost book and a hot cup of cocoa bring Emmy closer to sexy book owner

Jamir Cunningham sparks instantly fly. 'More to Love' is a short and sweet cozy interracial romance.

RIAN FOX

The Devil's Bargain

When a rare first edition book from a famous 19th century Spirtualist ends up in Silas lap at an auction, life as he knows it suddenly changes. Pressured into performing one of the rituals from the book by a friend, Silas gets a tease of regret. Now Silas can't sleep, is having nightmares that end with him waking up terrified. Something obscene, dark and deadly wants Silas and he isn't human.

Bazaduil lusts for Silas and won't take no for an answer, even if it means tricking and seducing him. In a life where being told 'there are no monsters,' it will be one lie Silas will have to face. Will Silas be able to ignore Bazaduil advances or will he submit to this demon's twisted agenda?

Support These Amazing Filipino Authors

As an author, it's important to me not only to write good books but to uplift other marginalized authors with the book community. It's also important to me to give back to the communities in which I take from. I am not Filipino and although I did my best to write Ichabod Crane's character with respect, it can not replace the lived experiences of real Filipino people.

Here is a list of a few books from Filipino authors you should read:

Heir by P.K. Reeves
Boracay Vows by Maida Malby
Wild Pitch by Cat Giraldo
If The Dress Fits by Carla de Guzman
My Imaginary Ex by Mina V. Esguerra
You, Me, U.S. by Brigitte Bautista
In the Warmth of His Light by Frey Ortega

Leave A Review

Thank you so much for reading 'Splinter'. It has been my greatest wish to get diverse LGBTQ+ romance into the hands of people who need it. Can you please leave a review? This will help boost my book so more people can discover it. It's a free, easy way to support me!